KRAMER V. KRAMER

AVERY CORMAN is the author of the highly-praised novel *Oh, God!* (recently made into a very successful film). He was an award-winning writer of documentary films and his articles have appeared in many magazines, including *McCall's, Redbook, New York, Cosmopolitan* and *Reader's Digest*. He lives in New York City with his wife Judy, and their children, Matthew and Nicholas.

AVERY CORMAN

Kramer v. Kramer

FONTANA / Collins

First published in Great Britain in 1978 by
William Collins Sons & Co Ltd
First issued in Fontana Books 1979
Second Impression January 1980

Made and printed in Great Britain by
William Collins Sons & Co Ltd, Glasgow

For my mother

CHAPTER ONE

He did not expect to see blood. He was not prepared for this, neither the books nor the instructor had mentioned bleeding or the brown stains on the sheets. He had been alerted to pain and he was prepared to help her overcome that.

'I'm here, honey. Come on, do your breathing now,' he urged as he was supposed to, the good soldier.

'One, two, three, blow . . .'

'Fuck you!' she said.

He wanted to be the natural childbirth team member he had taken the course to be, the helpmate without whom none of it would be possible, but by the time they let him into the room, they had started without him. Joanna moaned random 'sonofabitch's', while in the next bed, a woman was screaming in Spanish for her mother and for God, neither of whom appeared to be at hand.

'We'll do the breathing together,' he said cheerily.

He was superfluous. Joanna closed her eyes to swim in the pain, and the nurse pushed him to the side so she could wipe up the blood and the shit.

When Joanna first presented her belly for him to listen to 'it,' he said it was a miracle. He said this automatically. The first signs of life had not really interested him. She was the one who had initiated the idea of having a baby, and he had agreed to this as the next logical step in the marriage. When she became pregnant only a month after removing her coil, he was astonished. It seemed to have little to do with him – her idea, her baby, her miracle.

He knew he was supposed to feel connected to the chemical changes within her. What interested him most about her new body was not the life within it, but the pressure of her belly against his genital area during sex. He began to fantasize what sex must be like with obese women, staring at them on the street, wondering if the gracefulness so many obese women exhibit is desperate self-delusion or the secret knowledge of indescribable sexual pleasures given and received. Ted Kramer, who never permitted himself to linger over the pictures in the lobby of the porno movie house near his office, amused himself by wondering about the financial possibilities of a porno movie, *Ted and the Fat Lady.*

Joanna began to stain severely in her sixth month. Her gynaecologist, Dr Anthony Fisk, who had been identified in *Vogue* magazine as one of the most successful, eligible young gynaecologists in the Western world, prescribed to Joanna, 'Rest in bed and put the cork in.' A discussion followed between Ted and Joanna as to the precise medical meaning of his advice. He placed a late-night, precoital call to Dr Fisk, who was irritated at the nonemergency nature of the inquiry and none too pleased to talk to a man, least of all about semantics. He said that his meaning medically was 'Keep her on her ass as much as possible and no more shtupping.' Ted suggested they change doctors, but Joanna was adamant, so they departed for distant sides of the bed, where Joanna remained for the better part of three months, successfully reaching the full term of her pregnancy.

Joanna did not express interest in substitute lovemaking during this period, even though Ted quoted from one of the childbirth books in which variations on intercourse were officially sanctioned. 'Intercourse between the thighs may prove to be an adequate, temporary solution.'

One night, after she had fallen asleep, Ted attempted to masturbate in their bathroom to the fantasy of a fat woman he had seen that day in the subway. He switched before orgasm to a fantasy of Joanna herself so as not to cheat on her. Feeling guilty anyway about his indiscretion, he sublimated his desires thereafter by throwing himself into the growing obsession in the house over clothing, mattresses, cribs, mobiles, night lights, carriages, and names for the baby.

Joanna's attention to detail on such as the comparative merits of high chairs with beads for baby to spin and those without far exceeded his, and he ascribed it to the naturalness of motherhood that she, who had never been here before, had so quickly acquired the jargon of the trade. He had difficulty distinguishing between *layette* and *bassinet*, since *layette* sounded as though the baby should lay in it, rather than be the baby's clothes, while *bassinet* sounded like something the baby should bathe in, rather than lay on, where *bumpers* were easier for him to identify – they went around the crib and had visual educational material on them, like bunnies.

Lady Madonna was the store where Joanna bought her maternity clothes, a name that seemed apt to him, since she had satisfied every notion of the beautiful mother-to-be. Her skin was radiant, her eyes were bright, a madonna and chaste, thanks to the wisdom of Dr Fisk. Joanna Kramer was nearly professional in her looks, too slight at five-three to be taken for a model, possibly an actress, a striking, slender woman with long, black hair, a thin, elegant nose, large brown eyes, and somewhat chesty for her frame. 'The prettiest girl around,' Ted called her. His image of himself was less secure. A reasonably attractive man of five-ten with brown eyes and light-brown hair, he was self-conscious about his nose, which he felt was too long, and his hair, which had begun to thin. An indication of his self-image was that he felt most attractive when Joanna was on his arm. His hope was that the child would not, by some unfortunate irony, have his looks.

He was solicitous during the pregnancy, he wanted to bring her spare-ribs late at night, run out for ice-cream, but she had none of these clichéd whims, so he often brought her flowers instead, which before this he would have considered excessively romantic.

Joanna slept peacefully for a woman now in her seventh month. His nights were difficult as he moved in and out of wakefulness, a vague disturbance flickering just beyond his reach.

Ten couples assembled in a Greenwich Village brownstone. The promise of the instructor was that the women could have control over their bodies, which was greeted solemnly, no one noting the contradiction of ten bulging women, some of whom were having difficulty walking, having control over their bodies. The men, for their part, were promised they could be active participants in the birth of their own children. The instructor was an enthusiastic young woman in leotards, the only flat-bellied woman in sight and when Ted, in the middle of a discussion about the placenta, began having sexual fantasies about her and her flat belly, he took it as a sign that his period of fat-lady sexual deviation had ended.

His dream belly then introduced into the proceedings a series of shocks to Ted's system. They were colour slides she projected on to a screen which showed the most graphic depiction he had seen yet of the development of the foetus, followed by pictures of new babies, awake mothers, beaming fathers. A real baby was coming, not a baby in a book or hidden within her belly, a breathing person, in his life.

The following day at lunchtime, while sitting on the steps of the 42nd Street Library eating an ice-cream pop, after having priced the birth announcements at Lord & Taylor and before re-checking the prices on cribs at Saks, the realization came to him, the flickering in the distance took shape. It was fear. He was scared. He was scared Joanna would die. He was scared the baby would die. He was scared Joanna and the baby both would die. He was scared that they would be all right, but later he would die. He was scared about being able to afford the baby. He was scared about holding the baby, scared about dropping the baby. He was scared of the baby being born blind, retarded, crippled, with one arm, or one leg, with missing fingers, splotched skin. He was scared that he would be found wanting, scared that he would not be a good father. He told Joanna none of this.

The mechanism he chose for dealing with his fear was to obliterate it. He would be Godlike, control everything, leave nothing to ignorance or chance. He would be the best-trained, best-informed natural childbirth father anywhere. In the weekly classes, he was focused and intense. He could practically scan Joanna's middle with X-ray eyes like Superman and see the position of the baby. When Joanna began to experience increasing discomfort in her ninth month, he was extremely supportive. They practiced the breathing exercises daily at his encouragement. He was a model pre-daddy.

At the end of the natural childbirth course there was a motion picture shown in a local school of an actual birth by natural childbirth methods. In the audience were all types of expectant fathers and bellies of various possible shapes. He felt a kinship with these people, smiling at strangers. The film ended. The course was completed. Ted Kramer was ready to have the baby.

'Will you be disappointed in me if I don't succeed?'

'What do you mean?'

'Well, I was talking to somebody who had to be put out, and she feels guilty that she wasn't awake for it.'

'There are no failures, like they said. Don't worry about that, darling. You take it as far as you can.'

'Okay.'

Just don't die on me, Joanna. I couldn't bear to lose you – which he could not say aloud. He did not want to frighten her, or bring his own fears to the surface.

When the call came, he was at his desk in the office, right where he was supposed to be, a ten-minute cab ride from the house, in control. It began to slip away from him at the start. He had not counted on the speed and the severity of Joanna's labour, and he reached the house to find her doubled up on the floor.

'My God – '

'It's bad, Ted – '

'Jesus – '

All the training suddenly went out of his head as he saw the extent of her pain. He held her until the contraction had passed. Then he took the bag which had been packed for days – he had kept his cab waiting – and they were on their way to the hospital.

'I can't stand it.'

'You'll be okay, darling. Breathe.'

'No.'

'You can do it. Please, breathe!' And she made an attempt at the breathing rhythms, which were supposed to deprogramme the brain away from pain.

'It's gone.'

'Darling, you've got to try to get on top of it next time. Remember. On top.'

'Maybe they should just put me out.'

At 79th Street and Park Avenue the cab was stopped by a traffic jam.

'We can't have this!' he shouted at the cabdriver.

'What can I do, mister?'

Ted leaped out of the cab.

'Emergency! Woman in labour! Emergency!'

He raced out in the middle of traffic, holding cars up, directing others, an instant, crazed traffic cop. 'Move that truck, goddammit. Let's break this up.' Hardened New York City drivers bewildered by the sight of this maniac responded. In a moment of grandeur, he was a heroic figure rescuing his pregnant wife from a New York traffic jam. They sped to the hospital, the driver leaning on his horn at Ted's admonition – 'Go through the lights. I'll pay the fines.'

His moment was over, having lasted but a moment. When they reached the hospital, Joanna was taken upstairs, and he was alone in the reception-room waiting, yesterday's hero. *They* were in control now, and they had her and were shaving her pubic hair away.

'This is unfair,' he protested to the receptionist. 'I'm needed upstairs with my wife.'

'They'll call down.'

'When?'

'It takes about twenty minutes, Mr Kramer.'

'These minutes are crucial.'

'Yes, we know.'

In the reception-room was a beefy man in his thirties, who lounged in a chair with the calm of someone watching television.

'First time?' he said to Ted.

'Do people really say that?' Ted snapped. 'First time?'

'Listen, fella, I'm just being friendly.'

'I'm sorry. It's – my first time,' and Ted began to smile at himself.

'Third for me.'

'The waiting. Just when you're feeling closest to her, they take her away.'

'It'll be over soon.'

'But I'm supposed to be there. We're doing natural childbirth.'

'Right.'

'Are you?'

'All due respects, that's crap. Knock her out, no pain, you got your baby.'

'But that's primitive.'

'Oh, yeah?'

'And don't you want to be there?'

'I'll be there. In a few days, in the middle of the night, I'll be there.'

They had nothing else to say to each other; Ted fidgeted in the correctness of his decision, the man relaxed with his. The receptionist told Ted he could go up, and he went to the maternity floor, where Joanna was theoretically waiting for his help. On the way, he went over the variety of tasks he was to perform: time her contractions, help her with the breathing, engage her in distracting conversation, dab her brow, moisten her lips. He would be in control. He would not even have time to be scared.

He walked into the room to find Joanna twisted on the bed in the middle of a contraction, and it was then that he received her 'Fuck you!' when he tried to introduce the correct breathing procedures. The woman in the next bed was screaming in Spanish. The nurse was pushing him to the side. It was not going according to the course.

Eventually, Dr Fisk arrived, tall, a full head of blond hair. His first words to Ted were 'Wait in the hall.' After a few minutes, the nurse motioned for Ted to come back into the room as Dr Fisk nodded and walked out.

'Won't be long now,' the nurse said. 'On the next contraction, we're going to have her push.'

'How are you doing, honey?' he asked Joanna.

'This is the worst experience of my life.'

The contraction came, he encouraged her to push, and after several waves of severe contractions and pushing, he saw slowly appearing a black patch, the crowning of birth, the first signs of his own child. It was all of it outside his control, awesome.

'Mr Kramer?' Dr Fisk had returned. 'We're going to go in and have our baby.'

Ted kissed Joanna, she forced a smile, and he went with Dr Fisk to a room off the hall.

'Just do what I do, Mr Kramer.'

Ted played doctor. He scrubbed, put on a blue gown. And standing there in his doctor's gown, looking in the mirror at the evidence of the charade, realizing how little control he actually had over any of it, he was suddenly engulfed by the fear he had been denying.

'Are you going to be all right?'

'I think so.'

'You're not going to pass out in there, are you?'

'No.'

'You know, when they first started letting fathers into the delivery-room, somebody around here came up with a theory. He said that after seeing their wives give birth, some men became temporarily impotent.'

'Oh.'

'He figured the men were either overwhelmed by the birth process, or they felt guilty about their wives' pain. You know, what had their penis wrought . . .'

Dr Fisk had an interesting washbasin manner.

'Anyway, we don't have any real proof the theory holds up, but it makes for intriguing speculation, don't you think?'

'I'm not sure.'

'Come, Mr Kramer. Don't pass out – and don't get impotent,' Dr Fisk said, laughing, his insider's joke going unappreciated by Ted, whose face was frozen with tension.

They entered the delivery-room, where Joanna lay without dignity for this peak experience. She was prepared as though for some bizarre sacrificial ritual, a sheet hung down her middle, her feet up in stirrups, in a room busy with people, doctors, nurses, and three student nurses who were there to observe Joanna with her legs up.

'Okay, Joanna, only push when I tell you then stop,' the doctor said. They had practiced this at home; it was part of the course. Ted was momentarily reassured that something was familiar.

'Mr Kramer, stay next to Joanna. You can observe here.' He indicated a mirror above the table.

'Now. Push! Push!' the doctor called out, and then everything very rapidly – Joanna screamed as the waves of pain kept coming, she tried to rest taking deep breaths between, and then more pushing as Ted held on to her, his arms around her as she pushed forward and forward. 'Think *out*, baby!' Ted said to her from the course, and she pushed with him holding on to her and pushed and pushed, and a baby was out crying, Joanna was crying, Ted was kissing Joanna on the forehead, on the eyes, kissing her tears, the others in the room, not cold observers after all, beaming, even the star doctor, smiling, and during the celebratory mood as the baby was placed to the side to be weighed and tested, Ted Kramer stood over William Kramer and counted his limbs and his fingers and his toes and saw with relief that he was not deformed.

In the recovery-room, they talked quietly – details, people to be called, chores for Ted – and then she wanted to sleep.

'You were fantastic, Joanna.'

'Well, I did it. Next time I'll mail it in.'

'I love you.'

'I love you, too.'

He went upstairs to the nursery for a last look at the baby, lying in a cardboard box. He was sleeping, a peanut.

'Good night, little boy,' he said aloud, trying to make it real for himself. 'I'm your daddy.'

He went downstairs, made the phone calls, and for the next few days, aside from visits to the hospital when the baby's presence was actual, while at work, while at home, Ted kept seeing the recurring image of that peanut face and was deeply touched.

He had not been the helpmate they talked about in the course, but breaking up the traffic jam was special, and then there was the moment – holding on to Joanna, physically holding her at the very moment of birth.

Later, when it all turned and he tried to remember if they were ever really close, he reminded her of that moment. 'I don't distinctly remember your being there,' she said.

CHAPTER TWO

They met on Fire Island, where he had a half share in a singles' group house, which permitted him to come out every other week-end, and she had a quarter share in a house, which gave her every fourth week-end, and with what was left of these arithmetic possibilities, they were at one of three open-house cocktail parties that were held on the Saturday of the week-end they both happened to be there.

Joanna was circled by three men on a crowded porch. Ted was watching her and their eyes met, as her eyes met with a dozen other men who were also hunting. Ted had been shuttling between a group house in Amagansett and the house in Fire Island, assuming out of the combined total of two singles' scenes he would meet a Someone or at least a Someone Or Other. He had acquired the beach equivalent of street smarts by now, which was to know where to stand and what to do to meet the pretty girl on the deck surround by three men and about to leave with one of them.

When Ted saw it was a person he had played volleyball with, he walked down to the front of the ramp to the house and leaned against the rail. He stopped him, exchanged banalities, and rather than appear to be rude, the man had to introduce Ted to his friend. She was Joanna and now they knew each other from the deck.

He did not see her on the beach the following day, but he took a guess at her being on one of the three busiest ferries off the island on Sunday night, so he sat at the ferry dock, trying to look like a nonchalant week-ender reluctant to part with the sunset. She lined up for the second ferry. Ted noted she was not with a man, but with two girl-friends. Her friends were attractive, which would appeal to Larry of the station-wagon. Ted's friend, Larry, was divorced and an old station-wagon was left over from the settlement. Larry used it to offer women something of value at the end of a week-end, a ride back to the city. Entire group houses of women could be given rides, Larry in his station-wagon looking at times as though he were chauffeuring teams of stewardesses back from an airport.

'Hello, Joanna. It's Ted. Remember me? Do you have a ride?'

'Are you on this ferry?'

'I was just waiting for my friend. I'd better see where he is.'

Ted strolled to the beginning of the dock and as soon as he was out of view, raced back to the house.

'Pretty ladies, Larry!' and he rushed him out of the house down to the dock.

Heading back to the mainland it was one of Joanna's friends who asked Ted the inevitable. 'What do you do?' He had not fared well with the question over the summer. The women he had been meeting seemed to have a rating system; and on a scale of ten, doctors got a ten, lawyers and stockbrokers a nine, advertising agency people a seven, garment centre people a three, unless they owned the business, which got them an eight, teachers a four, and all others including 'What exactly is that?'s, which was often Ted, got no more than a two. If he had to explain further what exactly it was and they still did not know, he was probably down to a one.

'I'm a space salesman.'

'Who with?' Joanna asked. He did not have to explain, a possible five.

'*Leisure* magazines.'

'Oh, right.'

'How do you know them?'

'I'm at J. Walter.'

She worked at an advertising agency, good and not so good, he thought. They were in the same field. On the other hand, she was not an undiscovered librarian from Corona, Queens.

Joanna Stern had come to New York with a liberal arts degree from Boston University, which she discovered was not the key to the city. She had to take a secretarial course to qualify as a secretary and moved from 'glamour job' to 'glamour job,' one less tedious than the next, as her office skills improved, and she was eventually executive secretary to the public relations head of J. Walter Thompson.

When she was twenty-four she took her first apartment alone. She had become involved with a married man in her office and a room-mate was inconvenient. The affair lasted three months, ending when he drank too much, vomited on her rug and took the train home to his wife in Port Washington.

She would go back every Christmas to Lexington, Massachusetts and file a favourable progress report, 'I'm dating and doing well at work.' Her father owned a successful pharmacy in town, her mother was a housewife. She was an only child, indulged, the favourite niece in the family, the favourite cousin. When she wanted to summer in Europe she did, when she wanted new clothes she had them, but as her mother was fond of saying, she was 'never any trouble.'

Occasionally, she would scan the want ads to see if there might be something else she could do in the world. She was earning $175 a week, the work was mildly interesting, she did not have much ambition to change. It was as she had said to her parents, 'I'm dating and doing well at work.' Events had become familiar, though Bill, her present married man was interchangeable with Walt, the married man of the year before, and of the non-marrieds, Stan after Walt, but before Jeff, was interchangeable with Michael after Jeff and before Don. By the time she was thirty, at her present rate, she would have slept with more than two dozen men, which was beginning to sound like more than she wished to think of for herself. She was starting to feel a little cheap and used up. She informed Bill, the current entry, that week-ends were boring without him and, baiting him, said she wanted to be invited up to his home in Stamford. Naturally, this was impossible, so they did the next best thing – they broke up.

Ted was not next. She kept him in a holding pattern somewhere over Fire Island and Amagansett. Ted Kramer had arrived at this point after wandering in and out of women's lives into his early thirties, as they had wandered in and out of his. He completed NYU with a degree in business administration, qualifying him to do virtually anything or nothing. He took a job as a sales trainee for a small electronics firm, went into the Army as a six-month reservist, and had a one-year career as a wholesale appliances salesman. He never considered the family business. His father was the owner of a luncheonette in the garment industry and complained for years, 'I'm up to my ears in chicken salad and garbage.' Ted did not want this for himself either. An elderly woman, an old-timer in the personnel field, gave Ted what became the most important advice of his professional life.

'Your big mistake is to try to sell products. You're not pushy enough.'

'What do you mean?' he said timidly.

'You're smart. You could sell, but not products. What you should sell is ideas.'

A few weeks later she had placed him in a job selling ideas, as a salesman of advertising space for a group of men's magazines. A salesman in this field had to know about demographics, markets; he had to work with research tabulations. Intelligence was required, and Ted Kramer, who was brighter than he was aggressive, had a calling.

Ted and Joanna finally got together after the summer for their first date, dinner in an East Side pub, spending what would be considered, in the singles' merry-go-round, a pleasant evening. They were on the scoreboard. They had seen each other in the city. A stockbroker, a copy-writer, an architect, like people holding tickets in a bakery, were all lined up ahead of Ted. The stockbroker worried too much about stocks, the copywriter smoked too much pot, the architect talked too much about other women, and Ted and Joanna found themselves with their second date. In this singles' scene, where anything imaginative would be noted, he did something moderately clever. He took her back to the very same place they went to the first time, telling her, 'It worked for me before.' He was reasonably amused by the singles' predicament they both shared, not as detached as Vince, an art director who had been standing around her desk and who told her he was bisexual, and not as desperate as Bob, a media supervisor who also had been standing around her desk and who was 'on the verge of a divorce,' a line which she recognized from Walt and Bill.

'What I usually do with someone I *think* I like –' Ted said.

'You think you like?'

'The relationship is young. What I do is ask them to go to Montauk for the week-end with me.'

'Don't you think it's too soon for that?'

'It could be a fantastic autumn week-end and we could find out we don't have anything to say to each other.'

'Or it could rain and we could find that out.'

'But think of all the time we'd save. And all the money I'd save.'

'I'll take a rain check.'

After a few more evenings together, he asked again, she agreed, he rented a car and they took a motel room in Montauk. The weather was clear, they did have some things to say to each other, and without banter, lying wrapped up in a blanket on the beach, they confided that they were getting weary of the singles' scene. They went to bed on this shared confidence.

The decision, then, was never that Ted Kramer had been selected by Joanna Stern out of all the others as the man she had to marry. What was significant with Ted was that she chose him at that time out of a somewhat interchangeable group of men she had been seeing as a person she might see more often than the rest. By the general standards of the world in which they moved, this meant she would sleep with him eventually, and by her own personal standards, she would not sleep with others at the same time. So Ted was simply one man like others who preceded him who became the key person at the time. It just happened to turn out, given Joanna's malaise with single life, that no one followed him.

They began spending extended periods in each other's apartments, halfway houses, less than actually living with – more than just dating. He felt that he had won the gold ring on the carrousel: this person – in his field, aware of his work, sophisticated about the singles' scene, exceptionally pretty, star of beach-house decks and Sunday cocktail parties – was his lady.

The summer was coming, a critical time. Joanna could sense the stirring in the loins of the married executives who were thinking about getting into position with the office girls, even as these men were packing up the station-wagons with their week-end underwear, their wives and their children. At his office, Ted had been asked to fill in his vacation schedule.

'We have a momentous decision to make in our relationship,' he said, and for an instant Joanna was worried that he was alluding to a much more permanent arrangement. She was not up to that part yet.

'I've got two weeks' vacation coming. Want to spend it together?'

'Okay. Why not?'

'Larry is putting together a group house. We could get a room. We could have two weeks by ourselves plus every week-end.'

She had never been to Fire Island or any of the usual summer spots attached, and neither had he.

'It might be all right.'

'Four hundred a person, full share.'

'You're a real wheeler-dealer.'

'I think it would be nice.'

'Sure. It's a bargain. I mean, now that I know you don't snore.'

When Mel, the account executive, wife in Vermont, stood at her desk and asked, 'What are you doing this summer and who are you doing it with?' Joanna replied, 'I've got a place on Fire Island with my boy-friend.' This was the first time she had used 'boy-friend' in a sentence referring to Ted, and it gave her pleasure to do it, especially when Mel quickly withdrew with an 'Oh,' and took his loins elsewhere.

Being together in a place where so many other people were on the prowl, where they themselves had once been hunting, made them feel unique. When they heard that a porch had collapsed at a singles' cocktail party practically from the sheer weight of all that social aggression, they were happy not to have been there, to have been at the house eating Sara Lee brownies instead. The singles wandering with drunk or lonely faces along the walks, looking for a party, a conversation, a phone number, the Sunday night ferry rides back, last chance before the highway, people trying to salvage in five minutes what was not found all week-end – made them feel grateful for each other.

The sex was gamy, salty, the delicious quality of always being on the sneak, angling to find the house empty. Most delicious of all was the knowledge that when the summer was over, they could still be together if they wanted to be.

'Joanna, I'd like you to marry me. Please. I never said that to anyone in my life. Will you?'

'Yes. Oh, yes.'

They embraced with real affection, with feeling, but beneath it all, with gratitude for being able to prove that they were healthy, after all, and whole, and for not having to pace along the walks any more with drinks in their hands, looking.

The baby had been crying for what seemed like two hours.

'Only forty-eight minutes on the clock,' Ted said.

'Only.'

They were drained. They had rocked, patted, bounced, walked, put down, picked up, ignored, strolled with, and sang to the baby, and still he cried.

'One of us should go to sleep,' Ted said.

'I *am* asleep.'

Billy was four months old. Long gone was the baby nurse

who handed over a child who never cried during the night, who never cried at all, it seemed. The day she felt, this other baby emerged, with needs, who cried – often.

After the baby was born, the family had descended, Joanna's parents from Massachusetts, Ted's parents from Florida – they had finally retired. Ted's brother and sister-in-law arrived from Chicago, the family came and they sat, waiting to be fed endless snacks and drinks.

'It's a good thing I come out of the luncheonette business,' Ted said.

'But I don't. If I have to feed one more person, I'm going to hand them a cheque.'

What they had been left with after the nurse had gone and the family had scattered was fatigue. They were not prepared for the endless output of labour and the exhaustion that comes with a new baby.

'It's been so long since we made love, I think I forgot where to put it.'

'That isn't funny.'

'I know.'

At first, Ted was concerned with the proper behaviour in his new role. This meant he would get up with Joanna and keep her company while she breast-fed Billy, so at times there were three people nodding off in the middle of the night. After nearly falling asleep in the office on several afternoons, he began to limit his middle-of-the-night assistance to mumbling as Joanna got up to do it.

By eight months, the baby was sleeping longer hours. The daytime labour for Joanna was still constant, though – washes, shopping, feedings. She knew she was supposed to look forward to seeing Ted come home at night because he was her husband. Mostly, she wanted him home to get some help – maybe he could sort the laundry, wash the kitchen floor.

'Joanna, I am so horny –'

'Honey, I don't want to make love. What I want is a room of my own.'

They laughed, barely, and fell asleep soon after.

They kept hearing from people that 'It gets better,' and

eventually it did. Billy was sleeping through the night, a cheerful child and beautiful looking. Ted's anxieties, right or wrong, that the baby might look like him appeared to be unfounded, since virtually no one was ever of the opinion that the baby looked like him. Billy had a small nose, large brown eyes, straight black hair, beautiful.

As their life changed, their friends shifted. Single people belonged to another solar system. When they were first married Ted had moved into Joanna's apartment in the East Seventies, which was in a building populated largely by singles and a few stray hookers. They moved a few blocks away to a family building, and their closest friends became Thelma and Charlie Spiegel, their neighbours from 3-G downstairs, who had a little girl Kim, three months older than Billy. Charlie was a dentist. A space salesman from *Newsweek*, Marv, with his wife Linda became part of their circle. They had a Jeremy, two months older. First-time parents of small children, they would sit over boeuf bourguignon and discuss bowel movements and toilet training, obsessed discussions of the comparative progress of their children – who was standing, walking, talking, pissing in a potty, shitting on the floor, and they stayed with it and it involved them all. Even at those moments when somebody might say, 'Hey, can't we talk about something else?' the transition was only slight and the something else was related — bringing up children in New York City, public schools or private schools, and occasionally, not all that often, movies seen or books read, assuming anyone in the room had the time to read.

Billy Kramer at eighteen months was a child people stopped to look at on the street with his beautiful mother.

At work, Ted had received a raise simply because he was a father now, he surmised, a member of a club. He went to Giants football games with an old college friend, Dan, a lawyer. He read news magazines and *The Wall Street Journal* for his work. He *had* work. Joanna's club consisted of a few park-bench friends, some of the less controlling nannies, and Thelma, nothing quite as colourful in her mind as

Ted going off to an office where he was with people over thirty inches high who spoke in complete sentences. And in her world there was no one, not the park-bench club, nor her old friends, nor Ted, no one with whom she could share the dirty little secret.

She did bring it up, but they did not want to hear it.

'I love my baby,' she said one day to Thelma. 'But basically, it's boring.'

'Sure it is,' Thelma said, and Joanna thought she had an ally. 'It's exciting, too.'

She lacked a forum. The women she knew were either not admitting it to themselves or were more accepting than she. During a phone call with her mother, she broached it.

'Did you ever get bored?'

'No, not with you. You were never any trouble.'

Was there something wrong with her, then? One night, after listening to Ted and a long account of something that was troubling him, an argument with a colleague at work, she said what she was expected to, he should not let it bother him, and then she told him what was upsetting her – it wasn't that she didn't love Billy, he was so cheerful and beautiful, but all of her days were the same.

'Being a mother is boring, Ted. Nobody admits it.'

'Well, that's just the way it is. These early years, anyway. He is beautiful, though, isn't he?'

He just did not want to hear it. It was he who turned over and went to sleep.

CHAPTER THREE

She lived with the secret. It did not get better for her. The highlight of one summer was when Billy made a doody in the potty. 'Yeah, Billy!' she applauded and Ted applauded and Billy applauded. You were supposed to reinforce the child. 'Make a doody,' he said a few days later all by himself and he went and made a doody, and when Ted phoned the house to say he had closed a deal, a monthly schedule, full-page ads, Joanna had good news, too. 'He said, "Make a doody," and he did it all by himself.' It was not even her triumph or her doody.

Billy was two. Joanna's mother would have said he wasn't any trouble. He was sometimes stubborn or slow, but he was emerging as a person, moving from the primitive state of sticking cottage cheese into his ears into a semi-civilized being you could take to a Chinese restaurant on a Sunday.

She let him watch television, *Sesame Street*, and he sat, blinking, not totally comprehending. It bought her an hour.

Ted was in full stride. Tentative when he was younger, unaggressive and searching, at thirty-nine he had evolved into a knowledgeable advertising man. The previous year he had earned $24,000, not a killing in New York, but more money than he had ever known – and he was on the upswing. He worked hard at being informed in his work, and his immediate supervisor, the advertising manager, called him 'My main man.' He did not stop for drinks at any of the advertising-business watering holes. He did not trade sexual banter with the girls in his office. He was a family man. He had a beautiful wife at home and a beautiful child.

Week-ends were easier for her when they did city things together or when Ted took Billy for part of the day and she could go shopping for herself or just get away. What was it like to bring up a kid in the city, people at work might ask him, and he would tell them it was an exciting place to be, which he might have been proclaiming at the very time Joanna was at home, trying to stay engaged while Billy was building blocks into a garage, 'No, play with me, Mommy!' fighting to keep her eyes open at four in the afternoon and not pour herself a glass of wine before five.

The pattern of their social lives was to have dinner party trade-offs with friends fairly regularly. The Women's Movement filtered through to them, there were some discussions about roles, and for a while all the men were getting up together to clear the dishes. Ted sometimes saw his old friends over lunch; Joanna did not see her old friends. She added

Amy, a former schoolteacher she had met at the playground. They discussed children.

'Ted, I want to get a job.'

'What do you mean?'

'I'm going bananas. I can't spend my days with a two-year-old.'

'Maybe you should hire some sitters.'

'I'm not interested in a couple of free afternoons.'

'Joanna, darling, young children need their mothers.'

'Linda has a job. She gets up, she goes out, she's a person. And I'm standing there with Billy and Jeremy and their Cleo, who can't wait for me to leave so she can watch *As the World Turns*.'

'Do you watch it?'

'Don't make fun of this.'

'All right, have you thought about what you'd do?'

'What I did, I guess.'

'And it would have to pay for the housekeeper or the sitter or whoever. I mean, we don't have enough to take a loss on your working.'

'We're already taking a loss. In what this is doing to me.'

'What are you talking about? You're an incredible mommy. Billy is terrific.'

'I'm losing interest in Billy. I'm bored with his dumb two-year-old games and his dumb blocks. You're talking to grown-ups and I'm on the floor building garages.'

'You know, you forget so fast. At the end, you were getting tired of what you were doing, remember?'

'So I'll do something else.'

'What? What would bring in enough to make it pay?'

'Something. I know public relations, don't I?'

'You were a secretary, Joanna. That's all.'

'I was not. I was assistant to the –'

'That was window dressing. You were just a secretary.'

'That stinks, you know?'

'It's the truth. I'm sorry. And I just don't see disrupting the well-being of a two-year-old so you can go be a secretary in some office. You're past that.'

'I am?'

'Look, when he's older, when he's in school nine to three, maybe you can take on some part-time work.'

'Thank you for permission.'

'Joanna, where is all this coming from?'

'Two years of boredom.'

'I'd like to know how other mothers manage.'

'They all don't. Some work.'

'Yes, well–'

'Well, what?'

'Let me think about it a little.'

'You're on notice.'

'It's funny, I was wondering maybe we should be talking about having another child.'

'You were, were you?'

'People say if you wait too long, it gets harder and harder.'

'Do they?'

'I mean–'

'I don't want another child, Ted.'

'It's just that you are so good with him. We're all good at it.'

'I can't bear to think of any of this all over again. God! The feedings and the crap all over again!'

'It could be a lot of fun. We'd get a seat on your bike, scoot around the city.'

'Why don't you rent one, Ted?'

Clearly, she meant a child and not a bike seat. She sought out her new friend, Amy. Joanna said it all in one rush– how she could not get a handle on it, she was bored and confused. Amy was the wrong person. Amy loved children, she loved being a mother, she loved the idea of going back to children in a classroom when her children were older, supporting Ted's thesis. The boredom is 'self-inflicted,' Amy said crisply, Joanna feeling as though she had just received an F in deportment. And then, self-righteous Amy dropped a bombshell. She had something on her mind, too, that she hadn't been able to talk about to anyone. Amy was having an affair. He was married. A psychiatrist. Joanna had only been on the other side of affairs as a single girl. Here was the first woman she knew who was married herself admitting to an affair – and with a psychiatrist.

'Are they allowed to do that?' Joanna asked, trying to conceal her awkwardness.

They said goodbye with hugs and kisses, soul sisters now for having exchanged confidences, except Joanna was not sure she had received what she wanted in exchange. An affair? That wasn't going to do it, she thought. It would be a different set of complications. Although the notion of hiring a baby-sitter so she could have an affair amused her slightly.

Ted would have said he was sympathetic to the Women's Movement. He made an effort to 'do his share,' as he regarded it, to call Joanna before he came home to see if she needed anything in the house. It was her house to run, though. He would assist with Billy, give him baths, take him for a few hours on the week-ends. She was still in charge there, however, to deal with his clothes, his diet, his health, the pediatrician, his stages of development – when he was to be toilet trained, taken out of a crib, given a bed. He was the daddy, but she was the mommy. He wanted to help. He felt he should help. What he did was just help. Billy was still, basically, her account.

For a while, every child Billy's age in the playground was pushing the same giraffe, then they were all riding the same motorcycle, and now at three, they were all going off to nursery school. Ted asked how he had managed to develop into an adult person without going to a $1400-a-year nursery school, and wasn't that a helluva lot of money to pay for a three-year-old to draw pictures? If Billy went, though, Joanna knew she could be free for a few hours each day. What she told Ted was that all the children were going, and if Billy did not he would fall hopelessly behind and would lose the verbal skills he seemed to have, never to catch up. Ted wrote a cheque for the Pussycats Nursery School.

Even so, it did not relieve Joanna very much. Sometimes Ted dressed Billy in the mornings and dropped him off at the school. But Billy was home by noon with what seemed like an entire day for her to deal with. All three-year-olds are that way, the mothers agreed, which was no solace to her when she had to undo the fact that he wanted his peanut-butter sandwich in squares not triangles, his milk in the clown cup not the elephant glass, that he couldn't use the colouring paper because it was creased, that his hamburger had too much crust, that Randy in his school had a yellow bicycle with a bell not a horn, and that ten minutes and $20 after the cleaning woman left, the floors were sticky with spilled apple juice. And if Ted grumbled that everything cost so much and the company wasn't doing very well and he might have to take a pay cutback, at least he had a job to go to where they discussed page rates and readership and not Jiffy, I forgot it should be Jiffy, Billy, I thought you said Skippy, no, dammit, you cannot have an ice-cream sandwich for breakfast, and yet he was sweet, too, and beautiful to look at, and this did not help.

'I'm coming, I'm coming. I was in the bathroom! Can't you reach that truck yourself, for chrissakes?'

'Mommy, don't yell at me.'

'Stop crying, dammit!' and he would cry more and she would hold him and comfort him, while no one at all was comforting her.

CHAPTER FOUR

As Snow White in the school play, she was Snow White with hives. As runner-up in the Class Pretties on prom night, she had hives. Her first time with Philip, a boy from Harvard, hives. Her parents were always there for her to buy whatever cashmere sweater or charm bracelet she needed to compete in the adolescent Olympics or to help subsidize her rent in her early years in New York. So they sent her cheques. In the middle of her third affair with a married man she wondered if this was a pattern and got hives. She spoke to her mother, her mother felt she did not sound right, and they sent her a cheque for $25 to buy something nice. Under pressure she got hives, and they had almost kept her in calamine lotion.

When she was first learning to type and take dictation, she would begin to feel the awful itchiness under her skin. She would break out, like insect bites spotted here and there, which would fade in a few days, embarrassing her that she got them again. She did not like to place herself under stress. She always kept a neat desk and did not like to fall behind and then have to race to catch up. She did not wish to extend herself too far. It was all right to be a secretary, if you were a good one. She did not have to be a career woman, high-powered, tense, eating too much like the woman copy chief, eyes twitching like the woman media buyer – it was all right. She did not wish to have hives.

'What's that?' Ted asked, seeing her undressed as they were about to have their not-so-frequent, maybe once-a-week sex. A three-year-old was so demanding. They were both tired so often.

'Nothing. I must have eaten too much fruit.'

Tennis turned out to be the antidote. After a few hours on the court, the hives were gone. After a few weeks, she had become obsessed by her affair with Messrs Wilson and Dunlop. Her parents had given her tennis lessons in high school, just as earlier they had given her piano and tap. She played regularly while she was in college, surprising her jock dates by getting the ball over the net. In New York she did not play very often, a few times in resort areas before she met Ted. With Ted she did not play at all. Ted rode a bicycle and sometimes went down to a local schoolyard to play basketball with the neighbourhood kids, usually returning tasting blood and still gasping, longing for his wonder days in the Bronx. Amy said she played a bit of tennis, she and Joanna bought tennis permits, and at Central Park Joanna began playing again. First they played once a week during nursery school hours, then twice, then Joanna signed up for a tennis lesson the third day of the week. She was elated if she played well, depressed if she did not, she took mental replays of her strokes with her wherever she went, her last thoughts at night were of points well played or poorly played, she began to watch the matches on television, her game improved, she was beating Amy regularly by wide margins. Tennis carried her through the spring.

Ted had been asked to take a 10 per cent cut-back in pay and limit himself to a one-week vacation while his company laboured financially. Joanna insisted that if she had to spend every day taking Billy to an empty playground in the blistering summer her brains would fry. Ted wanted to be understanding, and they agreed to make the money available for Billy to attend a summer play-group at his nursery school. They would take a modest one-week trip to the country in August, but Joanna would have to give up the expense of tennis lessons. She still had her regular games, though, and with Billy away in the mornings, she joined a daily doubles group with Amy and two other women from the nursery school. She was tanned, trim, with her tennis whites, her hair in place with a designer scarf, pom-pom socks, and Adidas racquet bag. Outwardly, at any rate, she looked like she was winning whatever she was doing.

Men were asking her to play, people willing to step down in class on tennis to step up their social lives with the pretty girl with the fairly good game. She was tempted with fleeting fantasies of playing a smooth set with good-looking Luis or Eric or Cal and then go back with them, still glistening with sweat and make love, and talk tennis.

The vacation week in August was endless for her. Ted wanted to talk about business, the company, would he have his job through the year. This was a difficult time for him, which she understood, but then it was for her, too. Why didn't they talk more often about her and how did you talk intelligently about minutiae? The accumulation of little details she had to deal with was dragging her down. He would have thought these problems were petty.

They had rented an inexpensive efficiency apartment in Hampton Bays, a middle-class resort area which looked promising in the brochure, but was heavy on boats, fishing, and mosquitoes. In strange surroundings with older children,

Billy was not adjusting; he kept circling around her legs like the bugs.

'Go play, Billy! Don't you have anything to play?'

'I can't decide.'

Decide. She wondered – did three-year-olds use the word decide? He was so bright, so pretty, such a pain in the ass.

'Go swim, then.'

'Jesus, Joanna, how can he swim?'

'You swim with him, then. I'm resting. Can't I rest?'

Her guys went off to splash in the pool and she vowed never to go on a vacation for them again, never to be where there was not any tennis.

Ted found courts. A local tennis club rented hourly time to outsiders during the week, with a baby-sitter on the premises, too, and hadn't she said she would play with him? She had taken her racquet, he could borrow one there. In the city he had referred to himself in front of people as a tennis widower, but they were on vacation now, she could spare an hour of tennis for him, couldn't she?

The hour was nearly as long as the week for her. Ted had played only a few times in his life. He was like a wild bear on the court. They were next to a mixed doubles game of older players. Ted's balls kept interrupting their game, he kept forgetting not to cross behind them to get his balls, he was slow in returning theirs, Billy somehow escaped his teenage captor and peered through the fence behind her with his dark eyes, whining for apple juice, they only had Seven-Up, he hated Seven-Up. She chased him back to the sitter, Ted lost a ball over the fence, put a ball in play from the next court. She was humiliated. He was a clod from neighbourhood schoolyards, crude. That night, when he pulled at her, she made love to him mechanically, waiting for him to get done.

The next day, their last, finally, she left Ted and Billy at the pool and wandered down to the bay beach. She sat down on a dock, staring into the oily water. Did they know she was gone? Did they care? She did not care. She could sit there for hours and not miss them. She would call Amy first thing back in the city and play Monday morning, she had lost a week, Ted probably set her back with his clown act. It was very hot. Was this the worst vacation ever? The worst time ever? Rowboats had been set out for guests. She found a dry boat and pushed off. She dipped her oars for a while and then pulled them in and floated. Motorboats would pass and she would be tossed around. She rowed to keep up with the tide, but largely she floated. When was the best time? High school? Having Vicki Cole's face turn red when Marty Russell asked her out instead of Vicki. Knowing then she was pretty. Where were they now? Was Vicki floating in a rowboat somewhere wondering what happened to her? College was not bad, some of it. The first year in New York was exciting, up and down after that, but all of it, any of it was better than this. It was so boring, and when it was not boring that was only because she was under pressure and fighting with Billy and even the fights were getting boring and Ted was boring and the vacation, a break from the boring, was boring. She could just tumble over the side into the water. Better than sticking your head in an oven. That was not for a hot day like this. Her parents would cry a lot, and chip in for the funeral, which they would see was the best. Billy would be rescued from having her yell at him. Ted would cope beautifully. He would re-marry inside of two years, a fat cow from the Bronx, who would cook until he got round like his father and who would make him happy by going down on him more than she ever would.

When she rowed back to the dock, she saw them standing at the water's edge, her men. They had a milk bottle attached to a string with bread in it and they were catching little fish in the bottle. They had not realized she was gone.

'I went to J. Walter today.'

'You did?'

'To see some people, ask around.'

'And?'

'There's not much doing.'

'Of course there's not. Times are tough. Didn't I just take a pay cut?'

'But they said they'd keep me in mind.'

'Joanna!'

'I wanted to ask. I didn't break your balls by asking.'

'Look, you want to talk about this, then let's talk. What were you earning when you left? A hundred seventy-five a week? So assuming you get that again, what do you take home? One-thirty, maybe. And how much is a housekeeper?'

'A hundred.'

'If we're lucky. So that's thirty you're ahead. And in lunches, say twelve a week, and carfare, five, and snacks, three – so that's twenty. Now we're in the black a big total of maybe ten dollars a week from your working. And that has to pay for all your extra clothes so you *can* work, which means just one sweater or one skirt a month and we're totally in the red.'

'It's not the money.'

'It is. We can't afford for you to work.'

'I need something.'

'And Billy needs a stable home. Shit, Joanna, a few years more, that's all. You want him to get all screwed up?'

In other respects, Ted was as flexible as any of the other husbands in their sphere, even more so. He took Billy to the park, he prepared some of the meals, short-order cooking from his bachelor days. He had moved to a point of domestic participation beyond that of his father in the old neighbourhood and the men of that generation. But in the one fundamental area of Joanna's working, he was, in Billy's terms, somewhere to the right of Fred Flintstone.

She brought up the subject at random times – his position never changed.

'Look, why don't we settle it and make another baby?'

'I'm going to sleep. You can start without me.'

She passed her time in logistics, shopping, cooking, buying clothes, bringing Billy here, taking him there. She played tennis. And the time passed – slowly, but it passed. She was thirty-two years old. She had a little boy who was going to be four. She was happiest with him when he went to sleep peacefully and she would not have to fight with him any more on such issues as how she fucked up with the peanut butter.

She found magazine articles to validate her situation. She was not a freak. Other mothers, a few of them anyway, felt as she did. This being a mother, staying at home was not easy. It was boring, she had a right to be angry, she was not alone in this. Living in New York City, they were the provincial ones, she and Thelma and Amy sitting around playgrounds waiting for their children to grow up before five o'clock and the lamb chops.

Ted knew she was restive. He believed he was helping by assisting around the house. He talked to other men, to Marv, the *Newsweek* salesman who told him his own marriage was shaky, he did not know of anyone's that wasn't. They were moving to the suburbs to start over. Jim O'Connor, his advertising manager, married for twenty-five years, revealed The Answer at the water cooler; 'Women are women,' he said, a guru with midday scotch on his breath. Ted did not have many arguments with Joanna – it was more of a frost that lingered. She was cross at times, too tired for sex, then so was he. Nobody seemed to be doing better. He met dentist Charlie for lunch, the first time they had ever talked alone and not about children. 'Joanna and I – it's so-so . . .' Charlie nodded knowingly. Dentists – solid citizens. He told Ted *his* Answer. He had been sleeping with his dental hygienist for two years, making it right in the dentist chair – temporary fillings.

Against all this, Ted was convinced they had as good a marriage as anybody. Perhaps it was his fault she had been remote. He had been preoccupied with work, been distant himself. She was still so beautiful. They should have another baby, which would bring them closer, as they were that one moment when Billy was born. And they should not wait. Ted and Joanna and Billy and another little beautiful person. They would be a real family, touring the city on their bikes, looking like an ad. The first years were difficult, but it gets easier and they had been through it once, which would help. And if they could get this over with soon, in a few years they would be out of infancy and they would have this beautiful family, his beautiful wife, his beautiful children. And so, to be complete in some way, to create a perfect universe with himself at the centre, husband, father, his domain – for all the old, buried feelings of not being attractive, for all the times his parents were disapproving, for all the years he struggled to place himself – he would have something special, his beautiful little empire, which he, in his self-delusion, was going to build out of sand from a sandbox.

'I want a Charlie Brown tablecloth.'

'Yes, Billy.'

'I want hats like Kim had. Everybody wears a clown hat. I wear a king hat.'

'Okay.'

'Write it so you don't forget, Mommy.'

'I'm writing it. Charlie Brown tablecloth, hats.'

'I wear a king hat.'

'I've got it. See the *k*? That's for king hat.'

'Will I have a cake?'

'Of course you'll have a cake. It's on the list.'

'Where is the *k*?'

'This is cake. Cake has a *c*.'

'Can I have a cake with Mickey Mouse?'

'I don't know if Baskin-Robbins makes a cake with Mickey Mouse.'

'Please, Mommy. I love Mickey Mouse. He's my favourite.'

'I'll see if Baskin-Robbins makes a cake with Mickey Mouse. If they don't, we'll try Carvel. And if they don't maybe you'll settle for Donald Duck.'

'Donald Duck is okay. Mickey Mouse is my favourite.'

'So I heard.'

'I'm going to be four years old, Mommy. I'm a big boy, right?'

Ten four-year-olds were coming with their travelling road show. They were in the same class at nursery school, their birthdays all fell at approximately the same time, Billy went to their birthday parties, they came to his. Joanna and Billy planned the menu together. His party was going to be 'fantastic,' he said, which meant pizza, soda and ice-cream cake. They located Mickey Mouse in a nearby Carvel, she got the little baskets for the little candies – once, at her agency she had organized an elegant dinner party for one hundred executives and their wives at The Rainbow Room. She shopped for party favours. She bought Billy his big-boy present from his mommy and daddy, a giant Tinker Toy set; she found matching Charlie Brown paper plates and tablecloth, and on a Sunday in April, with Ted nearby to wipe up the stains, the munchkins came and wrecked the house, little Mimi Aronson, who was allergic to chocolate and did not say so, broke out from M&M's on the spot, and alongside her Joanna Kramer had hives again.

'Ted, this is no time to play with a dump truck. We're cleaning up.'

'I was just looking. Don't be so tense, for crying out loud.'

'It's eleven o'clock at night. I want to get to sleep.'

'I'll finish.'

'No, you won't. I don't like the way you clean.'

'It's good I'm not a cleaning woman.'

'You don't have to be. I am.'

'Joanna, think about the good part. It was a wonderful party.'

'It should have been. I worked my ass off.'

'Look –'

'You think all this got done by magic? The perfect little baskets and the goddamn Charlie Brown motif? I spent three days on this fucking party.'

'Billy was really happy.'

'I know. He got his Mickey Mouse cake.'

'Joanna –'

'I do terrific parties for kids. That's what I do, terrific parties for kids.'

'Let's go to bed.'

'Sure. All this can wait until the morning. I'll be here to do it.'

They fell asleep wordlessly. She got up in the night and went into Billy's room, where he was sleeping with his 'people,' as he called them, a Teddy bear, a dog and a Raggedy Andy. On the floor were the spoils of the day, the giant Tinker Toys, the dominoes, the Tonka Truck and the bowling game that came with the victory of being four years old. She wanted to wake him and say, Billy, Billy, don't be four, be one, and we'll start all over and I'll play with you and we'll laugh and I won't yell so much and we won't fight so much, and I'll hug you and I'll kiss you and I'll love you very much, and the terrible two's won't be terrible, and I'll be a sweet mommy, and three will be wonderful, and four, by the time we get to four, you will be my little man and you'll hold my hand on the street and we'll chatter away about everything, and I won't be perfect, I can't be perfect, but I won't be mean, Billy, not so mean, and I'll care more and I'll love you more and we'll have so much fun – I'll really try, if we could just start over, Billy. But she went into the kitchen so she would not wake him with her crying.

She began to keep score on herself. Every time she was cross with him or annoyed, which was inevitable, given the sheer mechanics of guiding a four-year-old through his day, this was proof that she was bad, and bad for him, and at its next level, he was bad for her. She began to keep score on Ted. Every time he did something inelegant like leaving a shirt on a chair, this was proof he was Bronx. If he talked about work, he was talking too much, the sexist. No matter how he might think he was helping, everything was still up to her, and the house – with the house there was no score to keep, The Peanut Butter Lady did it all, and every chore, every day's shopping, every roll of toilet paper replaced became a personal insult to her. And the dinner parties, still another, their turn, it was on her to do it, plan the menu, buy the food, cook the meal – Ted served drinks, big deal, and Billy waking in the night, asking for juice, Ted sleeping through it, all on her, the pressure, the awful pressure to get past each day, the hives not going away this time, as she lay awake nights, scratching them until they bled.

Into this, Ted came bearing his vision. Ironic, how unenthusiastic he was the first time, he said. He knew how difficult it was to be a mother. He would help even more now. It had not been wonderful for them, but they could be closer with a baby.

'Remember that incredible moment when Billy was born

and I was holding on to you, rooting for you?'

'You were?'

'Of course! I was holding on to you and you were pushing.'

'Really? I don't distinctly remember your being there.'

He was not thrown.

'Joanna, we're good at babies.'

'Yes, you're a good father, Ted.'

She believed this. He was good with Billy. But what was he saying? Another baby? How could he be thinking it? Everything was pressing in on her. And the itching.

She thought at first she would leave him a note. She could take time to organize her thoughts. She even questioned whether she should write it out by hand in a personalized way or type it. Typing it would be clearer, but not as personal. Then she considered a short note mailed without a forwarding address after she was gone. She owed him more, she finally decided, the courtesy of a confrontation, a brief question-and-answer period.

Billy had gone to sleep with his people. She and Ted were about to clear the dishes, hamburgers, the thirtieth hamburgers of the year.

'Ted, I'm leaving you.'

'*What?*'

'I'm suffocating here.'

'You're what?'

'I said – I'm leaving you.'

'I don't understand.'

'I guess you don't. I'll start again. Ted, I'm leaving you. Do you get it now?'

'Is this some kind of joke?'

'Hah, hah.'

'Joanna?'

'The marriage is over.'

'I don't believe this.'

'Why don't you start believing it?'

'We were just talking about having another baby.'

'*You* were.'

'Joanna, we've had problems. But everybody has problems.'

'I don't care about everybody.'

'We don't even fight that much.'

'We don't have anything in common. Nothing. Except for bills, dinner parties and a little screwing.'

'I don't get it.'

'You don't have to.'

'What is this? Christ, what have I done wrong?'

'A woman has to be her own person.'

'Agreed. So?'

'So I'm suffocating. I have to leave.'

'This is crazy. I don't accept this.'

'Don't you?'

'I won't let you.'

'Really? In about five minutes, I will be gone whether you accept it or not.'

'You don't do it this way, Joanna. Not like this.'

'Why not?'

'You do something else first. We should talk to somebody, see somebody.'

'I know about therapists. Most of them are middle-class people with a personal stake in marriage.'

'What are you saying?'

'I said it. I've got to get out. I'm getting out.'

'Joanna – '

'Feminists will applaud me.'

'What feminists? I don't see any feminists.'

'I'm going, Ted.'

'To where, for crying out loud?'

'I don't know.'

'You don't know?'

'It doesn't even matter.'

'*What?*'

'That's right. Is it getting through to you?'

'Joanna, I hear this happening to other people. I don't believe it's happening to us. Not like this. You just don't make an announcement like this.'

'What difference does it make how I tell you? I was

going to leave a note. Maybe I should have.'

'What are we, in grade school? You're breaking up with your old Valentine chum? We're married people!'

'I don't love you, Ted. I hate my life. I hate being here. I'm under so much pressure I think my head is going to explode.'

'Joanna – '

'I don't want to be here another day, not another minute.'

'I'll get the name of somebody. A marriage counsellor, somebody. There's a more rational way of dealing with this.'

'You're not hearing me, Ted. You never hear me. I'm going. I've gone already.'

'Listen, I think sometimes I've been too involved with work. And my mind's been on that. I'm sorry for it.'

'Ted, that's nothing. It doesn't mean anything. This has nothing to do with where you are – it's me. I can't live like this. I'm finished with it. I need a new place for myself.'

'So what are we supposed to do? I mean, how do you do this? Am I supposed to move out? Is there another guy? Does he move in?'

'You don't understand anything, do you?'

'I mean, you have all this worked out. What do we do, goddammit?'

'I take my bags, which are packed, and two thousand dollars from our joint savings account, and I leave.'

'You leave? What about Billy? Do we wake him? Are his bags packed?'

For the first time in this, she faltered.

'No . . . I . . . don't want Billy. I'm not taking Billy. He'll be better off without me.'

'Christ, Joanna! Joanna!'

She could not say another word. She walked into the bedroom, picked up her suitcase and her racquet bag, walked to the front door, opened it and left. Ted stood there, watching. He was bewildered. He seriously thought she would be back in an hour.

CHAPTER FIVE

He fell asleep near five in the morning realizing there would be no key in the door or phone call with an apology— I'll be right there, I love you. At seven-fifteen he heard voices in the house. Joanna? No. Batman and Robin. Billy's Batman and Robin alarm clock went off with the recorded voices of the dynamic duo: 'Jumping Jehosophat, Batman, we're needed again.' 'Right, Robin. We have to wake our friends.' For what? To begin where? She had left this with him and now he had to tell Billy. Tell him what?

'Where's Mommy?' He could not avoid it even thirty seconds into the day.

'Well, last night Mommy and Daddy had an argument . . .' Was this even true? he wondered. Had they argued? 'And Mommy decided she wants to go away for a little while to be really angry. You know, how sometimes you get angry and you slam your door and you don't want anybody to come in?'

'I was angry when Mommy wouldn't let me have a cookie.'

'Right.'

'So I'm going to take you to school today.'

'And I slammed the door and I didn't let her come in.'

'Right, just like that. Mommy is angry at Daddy and she wants some time to be private.'

'Oh. When will Mommy be back?'

'I'm not sure.'

'Will she pick me up at school?'

They were now but a minute into the day and it was already complicated.

'I will or Thelma will.'

He helped Billy get dressed, made breakfast and walked him to nursery school, where the Pussycats were having a circus day and Billy would be fully protected from his parents' world and happy, as any designated lion tamer would be. Ted was uncertain whether to sit by the phone, go to work, call the police, kick tyres, get an afternoon sitter for Billy. My wife has left me. It was unreal.

He always had difficulty with white lies. He never called in sick at work to sneak a three-day week-end. He believed if you lied, you were bad, and you should be good, and even now, knowing he could never show up for work that day, he did not want to lie. But you don't call your office in the same tone of voice as if you were announcing the flu and say, 'I won't be in today. My wife just walked out on me.' He called his secretary and said, 'Tell Jim I'm not feeling well,' which was true. 'What's wrong?' she asked. 'I don't know for sure,' also true to some extent. He just could not lie to his secretary and claim he was sick, and yet he could, in part, lie to himself as he had in convincing himself that his marriage had been healthy enough.

He called his neighbour, Thelma, and asked her to pick up Billy at school and keep him with her daughter, Kim. She said this was fine – what was happening? He would explain later. Billy was to stay there for dinner. He now had until seven that night to wait for Joanna to come home so they could forgive each other.

What you were supposed to do, it seemed to him, was call a buddy. Hey, help. Something shitty happened. You won't believe this . . . He did not know whom to call. He was suddenly aware of how isolated he had become in marriage. He had no friends. He had dinner party friendships. He did not have a buddy. There was dentist Charlie, who did not seem to be listening the last time they talked and who was more interested in revealing to him with sly pride how he was making it in his dentist chair. Marv, the *Newsweek* salesman, was not a friend. He saw Dan at football games. The deepest conversations they ever had were on the strengths and weaknesses of interior linemen for the football Giants. He and Larry had drifted since Fire Island days. Larry was still cruising in his girlmobile. He bought a new car and by choice selected a station-wagon for the transporting of women across resort lines. Ted's brother,

Ralph, was never a buddy. Ralph was in Chicago and called for an evening when he came to New York. They did not ask each other for anything all year and consulted briefly on an anniversary gift for their parents so there would not be duplication, the big brother who made a lot of money in the liquor business and wasn't there. Once he had buddies in the old neighbourhood, and then in college – he had met Larry and Dan then, and over his bachelor years, people from various jobs who were friends for a while, but they were gone. He had moved into an enclave of similarly married couples, and there was not another man he regularly talked to.

Needing to tell somebody, he called Larry. He reached him at the real estate office where Larry worked.

'Ted, baby, how are you?'

'Not so good. Joanna just walked out on me. Just left. Walked out on me and our little boy.'

'Why, man?'

'I'm not a hundred per cent sure.'

'What's your plan?'

'I don't have one.'

'Where is she?'

'I don't know.'

'She just split?'

'It was very sudden.'

'Is there a fella?'

'I don't think so. Feminists will applaud her.'

'What?'

'That's what she said.'

'She left you with the kid! What are you going to do?'

'I don't know.'

'What can I do for you? Want me to come over?'

'I'll let you know. Thanks, Larry.'

It was not very satisfactory, but he had unburdened himself a little, and in emotional and physical exhaustion he passed out for a few hours only to awake with a jolt; as with a vile headache a person tries to sleep away and it returns the moment he opens his eyes, he opened his eyes and his wife had still left him with the child.

If he could only get to Friday and then to the week-end, maybe she would be back or call perhaps. After Thelma brought Billy back, he put him to sleep with extra care, reading him several stories. Joanna's name did not come up.

He made the same arrangement for Thelma to take care of Billy on Friday, and owing her an explanation by now, said that he and Joanna had had a 'falling out,' his discreet usage. Joanna was 'taking a few days by herself.' 'I understand,' Thelma said. He called the office and repeated his not-feeling-well line and wrote down his phone calls – nothing from Joanna. He waited for the mail, there were only bills. He waited by the phone and when it rang he jumped to hear that Teleprompter wanted to sell him cable television he already had, and Larry wanted to sell him what he did not need.

'How you doing, Ted, baby?'

'So-so.'

'I told this chick the story. She went nuts with compassion. Why don't you get a sitter for the kid tonight –'

'No, I've got to stick around.'

' – then I'll bring her by, we'll have some drinks, and then you give me a wink and I'll leave like in the old days.'

'I don't think so, Larry, but thanks.'

'She loves to save people. She's like The Screwing Nun.'

'I'll call you, Larry.'

In one day, Ted was already gossip on the singles' grapevine.

At night, Ted and Billy followed the adventures of Babar the Elephant to New York, to Washington, to another planet. Was Joanna in any of these places? And weary from Babar's travels, Ted turned out the light. A half-hour later, when Ted thought Billy had already gone to sleep, he called out from his room.

'Daddy, when is my mommy coming back?'

Why were children always so damn direct? he wondered.

'I don't know, Billy. We'll figure something out.'

'What, Daddy?'

'We'll see. Go to sleep. Tomorrow is Saturday. We'll go on the bike to the zoo and have fun. Think about that –'

'Can I have pizza?'

'You can have pizza.'

'Good.'

The boy fell asleep content. They went to the zoo and Billy had an outstanding day, conning the pizza out of his father by eleven in the morning. He got a pony cart ride, a carrousel ride, they went to a local playground, he climbed, made a friend. Then Ted took Billy out for Chinese food for dinner. Ted was treading water. He was going to have to deal with this, make some decisions. He could play this out for another day perhaps and then it was Monday, he had a job to be at – unless he took some vacation days to gain more time. Joanna could come back, call.

At eight in the morning on Sunday, the mailman came with a special delivery letter. It was for Billy with no return address. The postmark was Denver, Colorado.

'This is from your mommy to you.'

'Read it to me, Daddy.'

The letter was written by hand. Ted read it slowly so that Billy could absorb it, and so that he could.

My dear, sweet Billy: Mommy has gone away. Sometimes in the world, daddys go away and the mommys bring up their little boys. But sometimes a mommy can go away, too, and you have your daddy to bring you up. I have gone away because I must find some interesting things to do for myself in the world. Everybody has to and so do I. Being your mommy was one thing and there are other things and this is what I have to do. I did not get a chance to tell you this and that is why I am writing to you now, so you can know this from me. Of course, I will always be your mommy and I will send you toys and birthday cards. I just won't be your mommy in the house. But I will be your mommy of the heart. And I will blow you kisses that will come to you when you are sleeping. Now I must go and be the person I have to be. Listen to your daddy. He will be like your wise Teddy. Love, Mommy.

Ted allowed for an instant the pain it must have caused

her to write it, measured by the pain it caused him to read it. Billy took the letter to hold in his hands. Then he put it in his drawer where he kept his special coins and birthday cards.

'Mommy went away?'

'Yes, Billy.'

'For ever, Daddy?'

Goddamn you, fucking Joanna! Goddamn you!

'It looks that way, Billy.'

'She's going to send me toys?'

'Yes, she's going to send you toys.'

'I like toys.'

It was official. She was gone to both of them.

On Monday when he took Billy to school, he drew the teacher aside and said, 'Mrs Kramer and I have terminated our relationship.' Billy was in his care and she should be alert to him in case he might be feeling upset. The teacher said she was very sad to hear it and assured him Billy would be cared for – he could be the cookie boy that morning.

Ted would have much preferred this day to be the cookie boy rather than the bread-and-butter man. He had his job to protect, especially now. Billy was wholly dependent on him now. If it were true, as he surmised, that his business stock had gone up when he first became a family man, did his stock go down now that he was a cuckold? No, a cuckold was someone cheated on. He was not that. What was he?

'You poor bastard' was what he was in his advertising manager's view. 'Just walked out?' Jim O'Connor asked.

'That's right.'

'She catch you screwing?'

'No.'

'What *she*?'

'I don't think so.'

'You're up a tree, Ted.'

'Well, what I'd like to do is take a week of my vacation now. Use my time to get organized.'

'Be my guest.'

'Of course, I don't intend any of this to affect my performance here.'

'Ted, to tell you the truth, you're doing fine. Better than the company. We may have to do another pay cut.'

Ted's face tightened. Did his stock go down that fast?

'But considering your situation, we'll leave you out of it. See that? By not getting a cut, you just got a raise.'

'If only I could go to the bank on it.'

'So what are you going to do with the kid?'

'What do you mean?'

'Are you going to keep him?'

'He's my boy.'

'Doesn't he have grandparents? This is going to be rough.'

The thought of doing anything except keeping Billy had not occurred to Ted. But O'Connor was a smart man. He was raising a question. Ted wondered if O'Connor knew something he did not.

'I thought I'd make the best of it.'

'If that's what you want.'

Was it what he wanted? He decided to follow O'Connor's question down the line. What about keeping Billy? There could be other options here – a way to force Joanna to take Billy. He would have to find her first. And even if he found her, why would she change her mind? She hated her life, she said. She was suffocating. Ted could not conceive that she would suddenly accept all the supposed pressure she was walking out on just because he tracked her down in a Holiday Inn with a tennis pro – he was begining to allow himself little scenarios about her. No, I'm going to have to forget Joanna. You sure came up with a unique little Bicentennial celebration, lady.

What about other options? He would not send a four-year-old to boarding school. The grandparents? It seemed to Ted his own parents had exhausted themselves being grandparents to Ralph's two children over the years. Ted was peeved at how little interest they had in Billy on their occasional visits to New York. His father would go into the bedroom to watch re-runs of *The Lucy Show* while in Ted's mind Billy was doing something spectacular like smiling. His mother was always holding forth about how wonderful Ralph was when he was a baby or how wonderful Ralph's children were when they were babies. If his parents could not stay interested in Billy for a week-end in New York he did not think they would have much of an attention span through the Florida rainy season. His in-laws were the opposite in abundance. They were pathologically nervous. 'Don't let him stand there, he'll fall out the window.' 'Mother, we have guards on the windows.' 'He's running a temperature.' 'No, Harriet, the day is running a temperature. It's ninety degrees!' He could turn Billy over to them and hope the boy would survive. Billy would certainly not fall out of any windows with them. Would they even care about Billy? Were they even Ted's in-laws any longer? None of it made sense to him. None of them could have Billy. He was his child. He belonged to him, that peanut face. Ted would do the best he could. It was what he wanted.

He met Billy at school and brought him home. Thelma called and offered to take him. The children played well together. It was no imposition. She wanted to know if he had heard from Joanna. He owed people an explanation, he thought, so he told Thelma that Joanna was not coming back. She was giving up Billy. Thelma gasped. He could hear it over the phone, a palpable gasp.

'Good Lord!'

'It's not the end of the world,' he said, giving himself a pep talk. 'It's a beginning.'

'Good Lord!'

'Thelma, we sound like we're in a soap opera. These things happen,' he said, although he could not think of it happening to anyone he had ever known.

The phone was busy the rest of the day. He had fallen into a pat explanation: Joanna apparently had to get out of what she viewed as an impossible situation. She would not seek outside help, and that was the way it was. People were offering child care, meals, anything they could do to help. Bring her back, he thought, just bring her back.

While Billy played at Thelma's house, Ted went through

the boy's clothes, his toys, his medicines, trying to familiarize himself with his needs. Joanna always took care of these details.

The next day, a brief note came to Ted, again without a forwarding address, this time with a Lake Tahoe, Nevada, postmark.

'Dear Ted: There is a certain amount of legal shit. I'm having a lawyer send papers regarding our pending divorce. Also am sending you documents you need for legal custody of Billy. Joanna.'

He thought it to be the ugliest note he had ever seen in his life.

CHAPTER SIX

Before he called his parents or hers or anyone else, he called Mr Gonzales, who was suddenly the most important person in the world to reach. Mr Gonzales was his customer's representative at American Express. The $2000 Joanna had taken from their joint savings account was the exact amount her parents had given them when they were married. Ted assumed she thought of it as her money. They both had American Express cards, but Ted was listed as the policy holder. All her statements came to him. She could have been out there, flying to different cities, signing for gin-and-tonics at swimming-pools, taking gigolos up to her room – and the bill would come to him. Now, that was a cuckold, he decided, modern style. He called Mr Gonzales and had their cards voided with a new card number issued for him.

Mrs Colby advertised in *The New York Times* and the Yellow Pages, 'Household help for discriminating people.' As an advertising man, Ted placed a value on the word 'discriminating' as meaning 'we charge more.' At least Mrs Colby did not also advertise window washers and floor scrapers as part of her personnel, as some of the others did.

He wanted an agency in the business of supplying reliable
people who did this kind of thing for a living. He was not
certain at first just what kind of thing this was. He found
himself involved in calibrations he never conceived of – do
you go for someone stronger on cleaning than cooking,
stronger on child care than cleaning? The advice of friends
was, You'll never get anyone good at everything, which
collided with his fantasy of a Mary Poppins straightening out
his life. He had rejected the idea of Billy's being in a day-care
centre. The day-care centres in the city were a scandal –
reduced funds, poor facilities – he would have trouble on his
income getting him in anyway, and he did want to keep
Billy's routine on some normal pattern. He went to see Mrs
Colby in her Madison Avenue office. On the walls were
letters of recommendation of people from UN delegates to
borough presidents of Brooklyn. Her office was tearoom
Victorian, and behind a desk sat Mrs Colby, a crisp woman in
her sixties with a British accent.

'So, Mr Kramer, was it a sleep-in or by-day you were
wanting?'

'By-day, I would think.'

Ted had determined a sleep-in housekeeper would cost
a minimum of $125 a week, which was beyond his budget.
A college student might keep an eye on Billy and do light
housekeeping for her room and meals, but this might not
be a stable enough influence. Ted wanted a substitute mommy.
What was within his means and more sensible would be a
nine-to-six woman in the $90-$100-a-week category – and
who spoke good English. Thelma, his neighbour, had advised
Ted on this. 'The person is going to be around Billy a lot,'
she said. 'You don't want him growing up with a foreign
accent.' Ted was amused by this at first and then he was not.
The idea was for Billy not to feel too different.

'Someone who speaks good English, Mrs Colby.'

'Oh, good English. Well, now you're talking closer to a
hundred-five a week than ninety to a hundred.'

'Just for a good accent?'

'For a good person, Mr Kramer. We don't cotton to
flotsam and jetsam around here.'

'All right, closer to a hundred-five.' Ted realized something had just been negotiated and he had lost.

'Now I've got to know something about your personal situation. It's yourself and your little four-year-old boy, you said, and you're in advertising?'

'Yes.'

'And Mrs Kramer?'

'Flew the coop, Mrs Colby.' A brand new way of putting it.

'Ah, yes. We've been getting more of that lately.'

'You have?'

'That's right.'

You would know, wouldn't you, lady, he thought. You've got the goddamn pulse of the city in this little office.

'We're still mostly your mothers-without-husbands, of course. On your fathers-without-wives, you've got your normal deceased, your strokes, your highway fatalities, your freak accidents – slipping and falling on your flights of stairs and in your bathrooms, your drownings kind of thing – '

He seemed to detect her eyes twinkling as she did her run-through.

' – your heart attacks, your – '

'I get the idea.'

'But we've had a few . . . "flying the coop," as you put it. One in particular came across my desk recently, a woman of thirty-eight, two children, – girls, ten and seven, – didn't leave a note or anything. Just took out her husband's dress shirts and eliminated her wastes all over them.'

'Mrs Colby – '

'Ended up institutionalized, so I wouldn't put that as a flying the coop exactly. More of a mental defective.'

'Could we discuss housekeepers, please?'

'I have three marvellous people in mind. In the hundred-fifteen-a-week range.'

'You said closer to a hundred-five.'

'Let me check my cards. Ah, yes, a hundred-ten.'

'Have you ever thought of selling advertising space, Mrs Colby?'

'I beg your pardon?'

'Let me see the people and then we'll discuss the price. After nine at night in my house. And I'd like this settled soon.'

'Very good, Mr Kramer. I'll call you later in the day.'

Thelma and Charlie came by, Thelma bearing a cooked roast beef. A slim, attractive woman in her early thirties, she was shored up by a combination of American cosmetics, tinted hair, contact lenses she squinted through, the latest fabrics, the newest fad diet – if it all slipped an economic notch or two she might have been just a plain woman, as she was when she was tired and the seams showed. She was unravelling now. Joanna's leaving had unnerved her, confronting Thelma with the problems in her own marriage and sending her back into therapy.

'I wish I really knew why she did it,' she said.

'Maybe she just flipped out,' Charlie offered, tiptoeing around so as not to step on any of his own eggs.

'I married a dentist, obviously, and not a psychiatrist,' she said sharply, Ted avoiding both their eyes with his guilty information about Charlie.

'You know, she talked about going out to work, and I said it would have cost too much. Now I end up paying for a housekeeper anyway and I don't have the income she would have brought in if she stayed.'

'That's pretty funny,' Charlie said. 'You pay if you do, and you pay if you don't,' and he laughed too hard at what was not as funny for anyone else in the room.

'Be quiet, Charlie!' Thelma shouted, and Ted realized that his own predicament had suddenly become a field for their battles. 'Can't you see the man is in pain?' she said, covering her own pain. She knows, Ted realized. They all knew Charlie was playing around.

'But why did she just leave? Didn't you people communicate with each other?' Thelma said in a tone rebuking the men present.

'Not very much, I guess.'

'Well, I don't mean to hurt you, Ted. So don't take this wrong. But I think she's kind of brave in a way.'

'Thelma, don't be an asshole.'

'Shut your filthy mouth, Charlie! What I mean is, it took a kind of courage to do such an anti-social thing. And I respect her for it in a way.'

'Thelma, I don't think she was brave at all. It's not brave to me to just run away!' The rage he had been trying to contain was leaking out. 'And that feminist bullshit! Joanna was no more a feminist than – Charlie is.'

'Leave me out of it, will you, Ted?'

'What the hell difference does it make why she left? She's gone! It matters more to you, Thelma, than it does to me.'

'Really, Ted?'

'The goddamn ball game is over. You're like the announcers who sit around the booth doing a wrap-up. So what if we would have communicated? The game is over. She's gone!'

'And if she comes back, you'll never know why she left.'

'She's not coming back!'

He lunged for the note from Joanna which he had left on a table. Gossip, they wanted? They could see just how ugly it was. He thrust the note at Thelma. She read it quickly, uncomfortable with the scene this had become. Ted grabbed it from her and shoved it at Charlie.

'Nice, huh? Is that a heroine? She's just a lousy quitter. And she's gone, that's all, gone.'

He took the note, crumpled it into a ball and kicked it into the foyer.

'Ted,' Thelma said, 'it might be a good idea – even if Joanna didn't want to – for you to see somebody. You could talk to my therapist.'

'What do I need a therapist for when I have my good friends?'

'Look, Ted, you don't have to get nasty,' Charlie said. 'You're upset, I realize –'

'You're right. And now I'd like to be alone. I thank you for the roast beef and the helpful talk.'

'There is nothing wrong with self-awareness, Ted,' Thelma said.

They said good night stiffly, Thelma and Ted exchanging kisses without touching. He did not want any more self-awareness than he already had or explanations for Joanna's behaviour beyond what he had. He did not want any more theorizing from his friends. Let them piece together their own marriages without examining his. He wanted only to get a housekeeper and have orderly days, a pattern, someone at home for Billy and the moment that was accomplished, Joanna would be dead.

Mrs Colby arranged for a Miss Evans to come for an interview. She was a tiny old woman who showed remarkable verve by talking non-stop about her dietary needs, Breakstone's cottage cheese, not Friendship, Dannon yogurt, not Sealtest, salt-free bread from the health-food store, not these breads they put sugar in. When she asked for a tour of the house and first requested to see where the bathroom was – she didn't have to go, she pointed out, she was just checking – even before she asked to look in on the sleeping Billy, Ted decided they were dietarily incompatible.

He located a Mrs Roberts who had placed a situations wanted ad in the *Times*. She advertised, 'Good cook. Good with children.' She arrived, an immense Puerto Rican woman, who conceivably had an agent representing her, since she had such a suitable ad, and an Anglo name like Roberts, while she spoke barely understandable English.

'I work weeth maynee Spaneesh deefomads.'

'I see,' he said, to be polite.

'Maynee Spaneesh esecutees.'

The plot thickened.

'Well, I have one little boy.'

'Your womeen?'

'Vamoosed.'

'Loco,' she said.

She pinched him on the cheek heartily, a real pinch. He could not make out whether it was an editorial pinch or a sexual pinch, but it hurt.

'You've taken care of children?'

'I haff six baybies. Puerto Rico. The Bronx. The baybiest, tweynty-two. He enyinee.'

If Mrs Roberts were employed, Ted figured Billy would be speaking Spanish by age five.

'You cude.'

'Excuse me?'

'You cude peerson.'

She was either making an improper advance or her agent had recommended the lusty approach. In any case, further inquiry revealed Mrs Roberts was not even free immediately. She was going on 'vacaytion' to Puerto Rico, where her husband currently worked for a 'deefomad.' By the time she had left, Ted figured out that deefomad was diplomat, esecutee was executive, enyinee he guessed was enyinee, and Mrs Roberts was a cude peerson, but he had not found a Mary Popeens.

He contracted other employment agencies, followed the newspaper listings and unearthed a few 'live-out' housekeepers, an attractive Jamaican lady with a lilting voice Ted would have liked to read him to sleep or other things, but who was available only for the summer, a stern lady who appeared for the interview in a starched white uniform and a starched face, a retired English nanny, who said several generations of children called her Nanny, but she wasn't up to full-time any longer – could she work two and a half days a week? – and an Irish lady with a heavy brogue who terminated the interview on her own by severely criticizing Ted for permitting his wife to leave, the woman having clearly lost the drift. Mrs Colby called and said she would make it her life's mission to find the right person for Ted within hours, since she had taken a personal interest in Ted's case, owing to his wife's unfortunate demise, somehow having gotten Joanna's notation mixed up with your highway fatalities and your drownings kind of thing.

Mrs Colby sent him four people, one in the $125 range, of which the lady informed him immediately and did he have a cook? Another, dizzily absent-minded woman who seemed quite pleasant but who forgot she had taken on another job beginning in August. A plump woman who giggled and who seemed as if she might do, except she called back to say she got a live-in for more money. And a Swedish woman named Mrs Larson who found the place too dirty for her liking, which made Ted uncomfortable, since he had carefully swept and mopped so that no Swedish woman would find it too dirty for her liking.

He was thinking about placing his own ad in the newspaper, but did not want to open himself up to the crazies at large. Instead, he taped a sign on what was the community bulletin board, a wall in the supermarket across the street. 'Housekeeper wanted, 9 to 6. Nice family.' He had heard this often enough. 'I only work for nice families.' He got one call from a Mrs Etta Willewska, who said she lived in the neighbourhood and had not done this work in a while but was interested. She was a short, wide Polish woman with a cherubic face, inappropriately dressed for her interview in what seemed to be her best dress, a black formal outfit. Her accent was slight; she and her husband had been citizens for thirty years, she said proudly. They had a married son. She had been a housekeeper for many years, then worked for the most part in industrial laundries. Her husband worked in a factory in Long Island City. She thought it would be good to work for a nice family again. She then asked Ted a question. It was something not one of the others had bothered to ask.

'What kind of boy is he?'

Ted was not certain. He had the general outlines, but he had never been obliged to define Billy's personality.

'He's very nice. Sometimes he's shy. He likes to play. He speaks well.' He did not know what else to say.

'Could I look in?' she asked.

They peered through the door at Billy asleep with his people.

'He's very beautiful,' she whispered.

The light from the hall fell across his face and he woke suddenly.

'It's okay, honey. It's me. This is Mrs Willewska.'

'Mrs Willewska,' Billy said in a tired voice.

'Go back to sleep.'

When they went inside she said: 'He's very smart. He said my name without a mistake. Many people cannot.'

Ted wondered about the burden of carrying a name many people cannot say without a mistake.

'I don't know if he is smart. At four it's kind of hard to tell. I think he is.'

'You're a very lucky man, Mr Kramer.'

He had not considered himself so over these past few days.

They talked in general terms about the duties of the job, which he said paid $110 – he could at least match what he would have offered through Mrs Colby. Could she come in for a few hours to get acquainted? Could she start on Monday? She said she would be happy to work for him and take care of William. On leaving she inquired as to the kind of meals Ted liked when he came home from work. He had not realized this was part of the bargain.

So he had a lady with a cherubic face who would cook suppers and take care of Billy. Trust your feelings, Thelma had advised on the hiring of help – and he felt he had his person. He called Mrs Colby and told her he had found someone. Adrift in her index cards, she said she hoped his wife was feeling better.

Now he could make his other calls. He had tidied up. He could say to his parents – My wife left, wait, don't go crazy, we have a wonderful housekeeper, it's neat, I made it neat. He could say to his former in-laws – Do you know where Joanna is? She left, you know. We have a housekeeper, wonderful woman. He could say – I don't need your help, any of you. I'm keeping him. We'll do all right. It's the way I want it.

He went into Billy's room and stood over him. What kind of boy *was* he? Could you know at four? What kind of boy was he going to be? What kind of life would they have?

We'll be okay, Billy. We've got Mrs Willewska. We've got each other.

The boy moved in his sleep, immersed in his child's dreams. He moved his lips, muttering words that were unintelligible. It was fascinating, but Ted could not watch, eavesdropping on his private world this way. He felt like an intruder. Little boy, don't worry. We're going to be fine. He kissed him and backed away. The child was involved in his dream. He was saying something about 'Snoopy.'

CHAPTER SEVEN

Nearly hysterical. Screaming. 'What do you mean she just walked out on you and the baby? What do you mean?' his mother howled, repeating it as though the repetition were required to record it on her brain. 'Just walked out? On you and the baby? Ahhh!' A howl from his childhood. 'What do you mean you got caught sneaking in the RKO Fordham? What do you mean the manager has you in his office?' The theatre manager knew the family. Ted's father had a small luncheonette on Fordham Road then and the manager called the store instead of calling the police. He and Johnny Marin were going to sneak in the side door the moment Jimmy Perretti pushed it open from the inside, crouching into the shadows of the RKO Fordham like commandos in *Commandos Strike At Dawn,* only to get caught by the usher and about to be sent up like convicts in *The Big House.* 'What do you mean my son is a criminal? Ahhh!' 'I didn't know you had it in you, kid,' his brother said after the manager released the hardened criminal in exchange for a hot turkey plate.

In the time before Billy, Ted and Joanna had gone to Fort Lauderdale to see Dora and Harold Kramer's new condominium, a garden apartment near a pool. While Harold watched television, Dora took them on a tour of the grounds. 'This is my younger son, Ted, and his wife,' she would say. Sons were identified poolside by occupation, daughters and daughters-in-law by their husbands' occupations. 'Ted sells,' she said, but she never mentioned that he sold advertising space, since she was still not wholly clear what that was. He would have been easier to explain if he were a big liquor wholesaler like his brother, as in 'This is my older son, Ralph, he's a big liquor wholesaler,' or a doctor like the Simons' boy.

*

'What have you been doing up there?'

'Breaking up a marriage.'

'I never heard of such a thing.'

'It's very modern.'

'Who permits such a thing?'

'Ted?' His father had left his game show on television, having delayed to make certain this was important enough to come to the phone.

'How are you, Dad?'

'You let your wife leave you?'

'The decision was not democratically arrived at.'

'And she left the little baby. Ahhh!'

He howled. The shame of this must have been enormous. He had never heard his father howl his mother's howl before.

'I've got everything under control.'

'Control?' his mother shrieked. 'How can everything be under control?'

'Mom, listen –'

'Your wife has run away from you –'

'I've hired a housekeeper, a terrific woman. She's raised her own boy, she's taken care of other children.'

'What is she?' she said quickly.

'Uh . . . Polish.'

'Good. They work hard. Ahh, what's the difference? It's a tragedy, a disgrace.'

'She's very nice. She's going to come in every day and take care of everything.'

'A disgrace. That woman. She's a tramp. A tramp!'

'Mom, Joanna is probably a lot of things, some of them I don't even know myself. But a tramp,' he said, trying to stifle his laughter. 'How do you get a tramp out of this?'

'A tramp,' she said definitively.

'A slut,' his father added for emphasis.

He had tried to make it neat. It was not neat enough. When he hung up he was still chuckling at how they possibly got a tramp and slut out of it.

She called him William; he called her Mrs Willewska. Ted called her Mrs Willewska also; she called him Mr

Kramer, the formality appealing to Ted, as if they were an old-line family like the Kennedys, accustomed to having help. She was a gentle, reasonable woman, intuitive with a child. For Billy, his mommy gone for ever was still an unfathomable idea. What was real to him were the details of his life, who brings me to school, who picks me up, who makes me lunch, when do I watch TV, who makes me supper, who does what Mommy did? These were tangible, and the possibility that these would be unpredictable was frightening to him. His mother's absence did not mean his world had come apart. No one to give him a peanut butter sandwich did. During the search for a housekeeper, these were Billy's concerns, which he verbalized with nervous questions about times of arrivals and departures for school, for dates, for meals – who does what, who stands where? As soon as Etta Willewska arrived, the unfathomable continued to be so – no Mommy? All else, however, was answered. Mrs Willewska did that. Within a few days, Billy was saying, 'Daddy, Mrs Willewska said I could not have another cookie. I had one before.' On a morning when Ted walked along with them to take Billy to school, Ted began to step off the kerb, only to be admonished: 'It says don't walk, Daddy.'

'We only cross when it says walk, Mr Kramer. So he'll learn.'

'Right.' Take *me* by the hand, Mrs Willewska and cross me.

She had brought stability to them. They were both, at the core, still bewildered. But on the details, on the peanut butter sandwiches and the walks and don't walks – Mrs Willewska did that.

To people in business he offered as information that 'My wife copped out on the marriage and the kid,' and usually said, 'But we've got it straightened out with this fabulous housekeeper,' saying this part so quickly he cut off their specific questions.

After several days of normal performance at work and the beginning of a regular routine for everyone at home, he decided to call Joanna's parents, since he had not heard from them. Maybe they knew where Joanna was. They did not. She had left it to Ted to tell them.

'You don't know anything?'

'Know what?'

'Joanna has left us, Harriet. She's gone. She's left Billy and me to go off and find herself.' You're some cutie-pie. You really left this for me? There was a long pause on the other end. 'I sort of hoped she'd have told you herself.'

'She left her son? Her own baby?'

'And her husband. She left me, too.'

'What did you do to her?'

'Nothing, Harriet. I didn't ask her to leave.'

'I think I'm going to have a heart attack.'

'Take it easy now, Harriet. Where's Sam?'

'In the back.'

'Go get him. I'll hold on.'

'I'm going to have a heart attack.'

'Don't have a heart attack. Get Sam.'

He guessed that a person who could announce she was having a heart attack was not going to have one.

'Hello?'

'Sam, is Harriet all right?'

'She's sitting down.'

'Did she tell you?'

'How dare you call with such a thing?'

'Well, maybe I should have written.'

'Joanna left her child?'

'Yes, she –'

'Her own beautiful little child?'

'She said she needed to do this for herself.'

'I'm going to have a heart attack –'

'Wait, Sam –'

'I'm going to have a heart attack. Harriet, you talk to him. I'm having a heart attack.'

'Sam, you don't have a heart attack if you can say it.' He knew this from his last case.

'Ted, it's me – Harriet. Sam is sitting down.'

'Is he okay?'

'We can't talk to you now. You've upset us dreadfully

with this news. You have a lot of nerve.' And she hung up on him.

During the week, Ted was usually home near six; he and Billy would have dinner together, he would give him a bath, they would play for a while, Ted would read him a story, and somewhere around seven-thirty Billy went to bed. It was a fast hour and a half. The week-ends, Etta's days off, represented long, unbroken periods of time, and anxious about filling the time and keeping Billy happy and occupied, Ted was booking up the week-ends with what amounted to package tours of New York City. This particular morning he planned to take him to the Museum of Natural History. The doorbell rang, and standing there were Joanna's parents. They entered quickly, scattering through the apartment like the bomb squad on a tip. Throwing doors open, they discovered one small child watching television and startled him with a cascade of hugs and kisses and colouring books. They moved through the rest of the house, and having determined the evidence first-hand, Harriet announced, 'She's not here.'

Sam prowled through the house again, as though he might find some important clue, looked in at Billy, who had not moved – *The Electric Company* had arrived with Spider-Man, which took precedence over grandparents, even from Boston. Sam clicked his tongue, 'Tsk, tsk,' over the boy and sat heavily on the couch.

They were an attractive couple. She was petite, a young fifty, dark eyes, her hair naturally greying. He had a handsome, craggy face, a physical-looking man with distinctive white hair. Ted had forgotten how striking they were. Clearly, Joanna was their daughter, Billy was of their blood. He would have been mistaken to think they would not care about the boy.

'What have you got to say in explanation?' Joanna's father demanded in a stilted voice. He seemed to have been rehearsing the line all the way down from Boston.

Ted recounted the circumstances of Joanna's leaving, trying to do it reportorially, quote her accurately – would you do the same for me? – and they listened, squinting their eyes as though they were trying to follow someone in a foreign language.

'She was never any trouble,' her mother said.

'Well, she is now,' Ted answered, getting in his points. They did not understand. They had handed over to him a beautiful girl, and this is what he did to her. They began to reminisce about Joanna's early triumphs, the pre-Ted days, oblivious to Ted sitting there – remember how pretty she looked on the night of . . . Then they would lapse into long silences. Billy called out from Ted's bedroom, which had the television set, to know if he could watch *Sesame Street*. The child, the child. They leaped up and rushed into the room, reassuring themselves that *he* was still there, kissing and hugging him all over again, as he looked up, confused by why these people kept coming in while he was watching television to kiss and hug him. They went through the house, checking all the guards on the windows. How would Ted manage? He wasn't qualified to take care of a child by himself. Who was this housekeeper? Did he know about the nurse who abducted the child and murdered it? Why was Billy watching so much television? What was he eating? Who would see to his clothes? He tried to field their questions. They were not listening to the answers. They kept looking through the house. Lollies? You have lollies? the pharmacist asked. Don't you know sugar is bad for his system, lollies bad for his teeth? They live in Boston, Ted reassured himself. They wanted Mrs Willewska to submit to their personal investigation on her day off. He refused. They wanted to take Billy to the zoo. He said that would be all right, but could they not 'tsk, tsk' over Joanna while they were with Billy and upset him? Now they remembered Joanna again.

'We gave her a good life. I don't know what you gave her,' Harriet said sharply.

'You may have just said it,' Ted answered. 'Maybe she was a spoiled brat, that's all, and when things got rough for her, she acted like a spoiled brat.'

'Don't you talk that way about my daughter!' Sam shouted.

'Shh. The child!' Harriet cautioned.

More kisses and hugs for a besieged Billy, and Ted sent them off to the zoo and went to a neighbourhood movie house, where he watched a Western, which had the virtue of having nothing at all to do with him. They returned late in the day, Billy sticky from a lolly, his shirt stained with pizza. Children – 2, Pharmacist – 0. They were going to stay in New York another day to be with their grandchild, preferring a motel room to Ted's couch, which he offered, straining to be polite.

Harriet and Sam were at the door at eight the next morning, ready to run four laps around the city. Billy wanted to go to the zoo again, and off they went to wake the animals. They returned in the early afternoon.

'We've got to trot,' Harriet said to her grandchild.

Trot, trot to Boston, trot, trot to Lynne, if you don't watch out, you're gonna fall in. A little children's game Joanna used to play with Billy. It flashed across Ted's mind. She had taken her clothes and left echoes behind.

'Well, if you hear from Joanna,' he said to them, 'tell her' – he did not know what message to pass on – 'that we're doing fine.'

'Are you?' she said. 'Do you really think you'll do fine?'

The investigating team left without a handshake for Ted. Joanna's parents had reached their conclusion. They had found Ted guilty of ruining their daughter.

In the weeks that followed, as it became clear to people that Joanna Kramer had really left her husband and her child, they began to read into it what they needed in order to feel comfortable about it. Larry saw it as an opportunity to get Ted laid. Ted told him he had no interest in a social life at this time, his mind wasn't in it. 'Who's talking about your mind?' Larry said. If he could get his buddy, Ted, running and chasing like he did, then running and chasing was justified. It was not so frantic as some of his women friends had been saying. After all, Ted Kramer was running and chasing.

Ted's parents were on the other end of the social spectrum. The important thing was for him to get married. They could care less if he got laid.

'We're not even divorced yet.'

'So what are you waiting for?' his mother said.

Legal proceedings were to begin. Ted had sought his lawyer friend Dan's advice, and he was sending him to a well-regarded lawyer who specialized in divorce cases. A quickie divorce and a quickie marriage to another woman, any woman, would go a long way towards salvaging his Miami reputation, and Dora and Harold's.

'A divorce, people could understand,' his mother said to him. 'I tell them you're divorced already.'

'I don't think they'll recognize it in New York State.'

'This is not funny. As it is, I have to make excuses. I have to say the boy is living with you temporarily while the tramp is having an affair.'

He spoke to his brother, more than miles the distance between them. Ralph offered money, Ted declined. Having offered the only thing he could think of at the moment, he turned the phone over to his wife, Sandy, who said she never liked Joanna anyway. She would have taken Billy for a while if their children weren't so much older. These amenities satisfied, they all said goodbye and did not speak again for months.

Thelma saw in Joanna an angel of vengeance for rotten marriages. She stopped by for coffee and told Ted that Joanna's leaving had forced 'certain things' to the surface.

'Charlie told me he was having an affair. He asked me to forgive him and I did. I'm also divorcing him.'

Charlie came by the following night.

'Thelma says I'm free to marry my dental hygienist. Who wants to marry my dental hygienist?' As he left, reeling from several drinks, he said, 'If it weren't for you, I'd still be a happily married man.'

Joanna's parents handled the situation by sending a continuous supply of toys, trying to make up for their own loss of Joanna with gifts for their grandchild, and by long distance phone calls to a child, unimpressed with long distance phone calls.

'Billy, it's Grandma!'

C

'And Grandpa! I'm here, too, Billy!'

'Oh, hi!'

'How are you, Billy? What are you doing?' she said.

'Nothing.'

'Nothing? My, my, a big boy like you must be doing something.'

'Playing.'

'Wonderful. Hear that, Sam? He's playing. What are you playing?'

'Fish.'

'Fish. That's nice – fish. What is fish?'

'Fish is I lie on my bed in my pyjamas and I make my penis stick up like a fish.'

'Oh.'

What kind of boy was he? Billy was an enthusiastic child. He could say, as he did from time to time, without guile, 'What a nice day, Daddy.' He was a lovely boy, Ted decided. He was not very aggressive, though, in the tough games children played with each other, and Ted wondered if this were a pattern, his own pattern? Was Billy going to be un-aggressive, like his father?

He was astonished by the child's imagination, tales of flying rabbits, and Oscar the Grouch taking a subway to Paris, sticks which became rocket ships, pebbles which became motors, make-believe so vivid Ted asked the pediatrician if he should worry about it. The doctor said it was to be cherished. Relieved of the anxiety, he cherished it, as he did their dialogues on The Nature of Existence.

'What did you do, Daddy, when you were a little boy?'

'I played games like you do.'

'Did you watch *Sesame*?'

'There was no *Sesame*. There was no television.'

He attempted to grasp that.

'You didn't have television?'

'It wasn't invented yet. Nobody thought up the idea of television.'

Something that was as real as television had not existed. The child tried to understand it.

'Was there apple juice?'

'Yes, we had apple juice.'

What is it like, Billy, to be four years old and trying to sort out the world? Ted wondered.

They came out of Burger King, a special Friday night treat for Billy.

'Did they have Burger King when you were a little boy?'

'No, Billy, no Burger King.'

'What else didn't they have?'

'Well, there were no McDonald's. No astronauts. No ice-cream pops you could keep in the house, because the freezers weren't big enough.' And no mommies who ran out on their husbands and their little boys, he said to himself.

The firm of Shaunessy and Phillips had been recommended by Dan, the lawyer and football Giants fan, who included in his recommendation that John Shaunessy was also a Giants fan. For the first fifteen minutes, Shaunessy, a tall, distinguished-looking man in his fifties, discussed Giants ball clubs over the years, presumably to establish rapport with his prospective client. Then they got to Ted.

'I'd say mine is sort of an open-and-shut case.'

'Nothing is. I could tell you twenty cases – open and shut, like you say – rattle your teeth.'

'Spare me, please. Did Dan fill you in?'

'Your wife took a walk. She sent on some papers and she's ready to sign away everything.'

'Tell me how it works. How long does it take? How much does it cost?'

'Okay, the first thing you have to know is, we handle both sides of the street. We've got husbands as clients, we've got wives. We've seen it all. The second thing is, divorce can be tricky. Right away I would say to you, you live here, *you* file here. Forget what she's doing. You can go two ways – abandonment. It'll take about a year. Too long. Or cruel and inhuman treatment – should be a few months.'

'Cruel and inhuman –'

'You'll see a doctor. He'll say you're tense. You're tense, aren't you?'

'Well . . .'

'You're tense. As for the last part of your question, two thousand dollars.'

'Ouch.'

'I happen to be, as they say, an old pro. I teach at St John's. I publish. I'm not that cheap. People charge less, people charge more. It pays to shop around, and I'd say you should.'

'I don't think I have the stomach for it, frankly. Okay, what the hell. Let's do it.'

'Fine. The thing is, Ted, you've got to have a good lawyer. Breaking up a marriage has to be legally clean and decisive. What we're dealing with is only your life.'

He was confident about the lawyer. But $2000 . . . He figured he got stuck by Joanna with the bill after all.

Billy's nursery school was running an inexpensive summer play group on week-day mornings, and Ted enrolled him with his nursery school teacher. The woman had been sensitive to Billy during the first period of adjustment and she told Ted she felt the boy was handling it very well. 'Children are more flexible than we think,' she said. Ted had slackened the pace on week-end sightseeing junkets, no longer feeling the need to book up every hour of Billy's day. A park playground a few blocks from their house had climbing equipment Billy enjoyed, a sprinkler pond, a view of boats along the East River and a truck waiting outside, ready to serve every canned soda, ice-cream and Italian ices need. Ted sat by himself reading news magazines, while Billy would make individual requests for a turn on the swings, for ice-cream. Ted did not wish to encourage him to play only with his daddy, but over the course of the day they would play together, with Ted the tallest person in the tree house or on the seesaw, or he would involve himself in one of Billy's games of imagination.

'Let's play monkeys.'

'What's monkeys?'

'You're the daddy monkey and I'm the baby monkey and we climb on everything in the playground.'

'Not everything.'

'The slide.'

'Okay. I'll climb on the slide.'

'And you have to squeak like a monkey.'

'Your daddy doesn't squeak like a monkey.'

'And you have to crawl on the ground.'

'Why don't I be a standing-up monkey?'

'That's not a monkey.'

They had reached a delicate point in the negotiations. 'All right,' Ted said. 'You do the squeaking and the crawling, and I'll do a little scratching.'

'That's good. The daddy monkey scratches.'

And they climbed the slide somewhere in Africa and were monkeys, or in Ted's case, a modified monkey.

On a July Sunday, the day was hot, they had gone to the playground with a picnic lunch, and Billy had spent most of the afternoon at the sprinkler, Ted joining him for a while with his pants rolled up and his shoes and socks off, as some of the other parents had done. Ted was sitting to the side reading while Billy ran through the playground, sprinkling water, skipping and chirping away, delighted to spend the day in his bathing-suit. 'Be my water man,' Ted said, and Billy would fill a plastic cup with water, bring it back and pour it over Ted's bent head, which gave Billy the giggles. They stayed late in the playground, and as the day cooled and the shadows grew longer, the park was especially beautiful. Ted was feeling a true sense of well-being, Billy was still giggling, dancing through his day. They had it all together, children were more flexible than we think, perhaps grown-ups also, he was thinking. He looked around and realized he had suddenly lost sight of Billy. He was not at the sprinkler or at the sandbox, not climbing, not on the seesaw. Ted began walking quickly through the playground. Billy was not there. 'Billy!' he yelled. 'Billy!' Ted ran towards the entrance of the playground where the water fountain was located, and he was not there either. 'Billy! Billy!' And then he saw him out of the corner of his eye. The boy had left the playground and was running along a walk in the outside park. Ted raced after him, calling, but he did not turn around. He kept running in his jittery gait. Ted ran faster and finally got a few yards behind him when he heard the boy calling, 'Mommy! Mommy!' A woman with dark hair was ahead strolling along the walk. Billy caught up to her and grabbed at her skirt. She turned around and looked down at him, just a woman, strolling along the walk.

'I thought you were my mommy,' he said.

CHAPTER EIGHT

Larry said it was the bargain of the season, a full share in a group house on Fire Island, a distress sale, the shareholder had had a nervous breakdown.

'From being in the house?' Ted asked.

'I don't know. It happened July Fourth week-end. She didn't meet anybody, and when the week-end was over she couldn't get out of her chair.'

Ted had qualms about exploiting someone else's mental condition as well as taking a share in a house where the occupants had nervous breakdowns. Under Larry's urging he decided to call the house organizer, an interior decorator Larry was dating, who had a ten-year-old boy.

'We're all parents without partners,' she told Ted over the phone. It made him uncomfortable to hear how casually she used that. He was in a category. 'We don't want any singles in the house,' she said. 'You'd be perfect. And you're a man. We want another man.'

On Friday at five-thirty Etta brought Billy to the information booth of the Long Island Railroad. The station was crowded with people fighting to get out of the city, on to the next train, to the suburbs, to the shore, and Ted rushed along with the rest. When he saw Etta and Billy waiting for him at the booth, the sight was so startling to him, he broke his pace and just stopped. Billy, this person who loomed so large in his life, this dominant figure to him, seen in scale in a crowded railroad station, surrounded by the world at large, was so incredibly tiny. He was holding Etta's hand, a very little boy.

'Hi!' Ted called out, and the child raced up and hugged him as if he had not seen him in weeks, amazed at the miracle that his own daddy had actually materialized out of the confusion.

Ted had always considered Ocean Beach on Fire Island to be over-populated and tacky. Suddenly, seen through Billy's eyes, with ice-cream cones for sale, a drugstore with toys, and a pizza stand – 'You didn't say they had pizza!' – Ocean Beach was Cannes.

He located the house, one of many similar bungalows with screened-in porches, this with a pink sign above the door that said CHEZ GLORIA. Gloria herself came to the door, a buxom woman in her late thirties, wearing cut-off dungarees. In the vogue of T-shirts printed with clever sayings, her T-shirt proclaimed across her breasts, 'Big Tits.' 'You must be Ted,' she boomed in a loud voice, and Billy tried to hide in the tunnel between Ted's legs. She introduced him to the 'housemates,' who were Ellen, a freelance editor with her eleven-year-old daughter, a psychiatrist, Bob, with his sixteen-year-old son who was with him for the summer, and a forty-six-year-old health food store owner, Martha, with her nineteen-year-old daughter. The house had a common dining-room/living-room and five bedrooms. The billeting provided for each parent without partner to sleep in the same room with his or her offspring.

Under the house rules, which were posted above the sink, each parent had full responsibility for his or her own child at the dinner-table. Housemates took turns preparing the meals, but no one except the responsible parent was to see to a child's fussy eating or dinner-time sulking. Parents were going back and forth running hot corns under cold water or warming up cold corns. Ellen, the editor, a six-foot-tall woman in her late thirties, watched the others to see how well her chicken was going over. The psychiatrist, a stoop-shoul-dered, austere man in his late forties, had little to say to the others. His son, a stoop-shouldered austere child, also in his late forties it appeared, also had little to say. The health food store lady had apparently discovered the nutritional qualities of her own wares – she was, at five-foot-one, about 190 pounds, and her blonde daughter was a few inches taller and a few pounds heavier. For dessert, they ate an entire chocolate swirl cake.

After dinner, Larry came by. The two friends had not seen much of each other in recent years, and looking at Larry again in the context of Fire Island, where they had once been running mates, noticing his friend's full head of curly hair beginning to recede and his middle beginning to bulge, Ted saw in Larry his own passage of time.

'Great party tonight. Great chicks.' That was unchanged.

'I've got to stay with Billy.'

'Bring Billy. We'll get him laid.'

'Terrific, Larry.'

'Sure. This is Fire Island, old buddy.' And he left with Gloria, who had changed her 'Big Tits' T-shirt, which became soiled at dinner, to a cleaner 'Big Tits' T-shirt.

Ted and Billy spent enjoyable days at the beach, Ted even managed a few volleyball games while Billy built sandcastles nearby. Larry phoned from Ocean Bay Park on Sunday afternoon. He would meet Ted at six on the mainland and give him a lift home, reliable Larry.

'One little item. Don't say anything about me to Gloria. We broke up.'

'Larry, how could you break up? You weren't even going together.'

'We did for a week. But where are *you* at, buddy? Did you meet?'

'I didn't look.'

'So do it! Go out there and touch a lady.'

Four months had passed since Joanna had left. He had not touched a lady. He had not touched another woman in the six years he had known Joanna.

'It's been a long time,' Ted said. 'I don't even know what grips they're using these days.'

Gloria rang a bell to assemble all units. She apologized

to Ted for the military aspect of it, but she rang a bell anyway. 'It helps keep the house together,' she said. So they gathered for the Sunday evening ringing of the bell, assembling of all units and the reading of the tally – total house expenditures, divided by units, less any unit disbursements. This was a part of group house living he had forgotten about – divvying up the money. The question now was, Did Ted want to sign on? His share would be $200, which Larry had told him was well under the market.

'I'm not sure,' he said, and the others stared at him, as though he might be personally rejecting them. 'I'd like to talk to the rest of my unit.'

Billy was outside playing hide-and-seek with a friend he had made from the next house. Ted told him they had to go home and he was about to add that they had to decide whether they wanted to spend any more time there, when Billy burst into tears. He did not want to leave his friend, his house, his island. Ted paid the $200. He was an official housemate, unit and parent without partner in Chez Gloria.

Ocean Beach was pulsing on week-ends with people cruising the bars and the house parties. The people in Ted's house tended to stay home. This made it comfortable for him. He could sit in the living-room with the others and talk or read, under no pressure to confront the singles' scene out there.

'I'm so tense during the week,' Martha said, 'I look forward to just relaxing.'

But Ted felt a tension in the house, which had been growing since the first week-end he had spent there, as Martha, Ellen and Gloria would make tentative forays into the night and come back early without having met anyone. George, the psychiatrist, rarely left his chair. Billy had made the best social adjustment in the house. He had a five-year-old friend named Joey next door, and they would play on each other's decks or ride little red motorcycles in a gang with other children up and down the walks.

Saturday night of his third week-end there, Ted was alone in the living-room with George. Both had books. He felt obliged to say something to George. They seldom spoke.

'Interesting?' Ted asked, an uninteresting opening.

'Yes.'

George continued to read.

'What is it about?' Am I really asking this? He wanted to take it all back.

'Senility,' George answered, and that concluded the conversation.

A half-hour later, Ted closed a book he was reading on oceanography and said good night.

'Your wife left you?' George said suddenly, surprising him.

'Yes. A few months ago.'

'I see.'

George seemed to be considering this. Ted waited. The man was a psychiatrist!

'I think' – George spoke slowly, he chose his words carefully – 'you should go out more.'

'I should go out more? George, I could have gotten that from my mother.'

He could not put it off any longer. It was already the second week in August. Billy was playing at his friend's house and had been invited for dinner. Ted had at least two hours to himself, and there was an open-house cocktail party on the next block. He poured a drink and headed for the party with his glass in his hand. As he made his way along the walk to the party, the ice tinkling in the glass, and others were walking ahead of him and behind him with their drinks in their hands, it all came rushing back at him. He would spot her across the deck, the prettiest girl at the party, and he would manoeuvre for position and get her name and her number, and they would see each other in the city, and they would go together, and they would be married, and . . . Joanna, Joanna, where are you? His eyes started to water, but he fought it off. He would not give her that.

Larry was there, his arm around another of his buxom discoveries. He waved Ted over to him, and Ted filtered his way through the crowd, checking the personnel on all sides as he went, an old reflex action.

'There you are, buddy. Ted, this is Barbara. And her friends, Rhoda and Cynthia.'

Larry's girl was pretty, heavily made-up, on the hard side. They were all in their early thirties. Rhoda was short, pudgy and had a bad complexion. Once, Ted would have merely dismissed her, because of her looks. Now he felt compassionate, because of her looks. She was on the meat rack here, as he was. Cynthia was a trace less plain, a frail-looking, light brunette with a slender figure.

'Ted is on the come-back trail.'

'Sort of.'

'I'll tell you something, girls, but don't let it get around. He was one of the best stick men in the business.'

They laughed, high-strung laughter. When Ted did not laugh, Cynthia stopped quickly.

'What do you do, Ted?' Cynthia asked.

'I sell advertising space.'

He could tell the non-recognition.

'When you see ads in a magazine, somebody sells the space for those ads to advertisers. I represent the magazines, and I call on advertising agencies and try to get them to buy space for their clients.'

'It sounds fascinating.'

'What do you do?'

'I'm a legal secretary.'

'That's nice.'

Barbara had invited Larry back for dinner, and now Cynthia extended a dinner invitation to Ted. He went back to the house and asked Martha if she would mind putting Billy to bed. It was fine with Martha, he checked it out with Billy, and Ted went on to the dinner party. The women had another housemate, who had invited a man in his thirties to also join them for dinner. Barbara's mother was out for the week-end and was trying to be younger than her daughter. She had invited two hulking men in tank-top shirts whom she had picked up at the dock, where they had a powerboat. The boatsmen brought their own beer in a Styrofoam case.

'I don't think this party is going to make the women's page of the *Times*,' Ted whispered to Larry.

'Wait until you see what we're eating. Charcoal-broiled eggs.'

Barbara appeared, surprisingly, with steaks for everyone, to loud cheering. The boatsmen took over the cooking. Ted and Larry made a salad. Beer and liquor flowed. One of the boatsmen turned out to be a football fan, and there was sports talk over dinner. Barbara's mother had made a pecan pie, which brought another cheer from the crowd. They all talked about food and about how wonderful they all were, and how they should all get one big house together. Cynthia was the quietest one there, as though in fear that if she said too much, she would offend the person she was with and he would disappear. She asked Ted more about his job, he asked about hers. Someone put the phonograph on with the volume up and Ted was at the kind of noisy party he had been hearing from his room when he was trying to fall asleep. He danced with Cynthia and she pressed her thinness against him, creating his first naturally inspired erection in months.

As the party became noisier, he took Cynthia by the hand and they strolled down the walk to the ocean. They stood there for a while and then he kissed her. She opened her mouth and they leaned against each other and he had his tongue in her mouth, and then he started running his hands all over her, inside her clothing, inside her. He led her off the walk and pulled her down on the dunes, out of view, kissing and fondling, as she said, 'Oh, Ted,' and for an instant he could not respond, since he did not know what the hell her name was, and he went down on her in the dunes, thinking you could get arrested for anything else, and while he was there, he remembered it was Cynthia, and managed an 'Oh, Cynthia.' A police car patrolling the beach lit the area with its headlights, and in the darkness it was as if floodlights had been turned on them, and they scrambled to their feet, making clothing adjustments. They went back along the dark walk, stopping every few yards to kiss. The party at her house was in full blast, the lights were still on in his house, and not knowing where to go or what else to do, they continued along the walk kissing. Ted feeling sad for her, how desperate she was to be loved a little bit, to be taken away from the deck, away from the party, even by someone who could not hold on to her name. They leaned against a fence in the dark, and he put his fingers in her again – tacky Ocean Beach – he felt as tacky as the town.

The lights had gone out in his house, and he took her by the arm.

'I've got a room.'

'What about your little boy?'

'He won't wake up.'

He sneaked her into the house, into his room, into the bed next to Billy, with the child snoring away, and trying to keep the sheet over them, so if Billy would wake up he would see a sheet and not a person – hopefully he would not think it was a ghost – and moving gingerly so the squeaking bed would not squeak too loudly, he kissed her a few times more, for show, and then entered her. He came in a rush, almost as soon as he was in her.

'I'm sorry,' he said. 'It's been a long time for me.'

'It's okay,' she said.

And there they were, pushed together in a narrow bed, hiding under a sheet next to a snoring child. Ted waited and then started to try again, the bed squeaked, Billy was moving in his sleep, and she had had enough of island romance for one night. 'You stay,' she said and straightened her clothes, which were never fully off. He pulled on his clothes, which were never fully off either, and because You Take A Lady Home, he walked her back in silence. The party at her house was still going on. He kissed her. She kissed him back perfunctorily and went inside. Within five minutes he was back in bed next to Billy.

They passed on the walk the next day, said hello and lowered their eyes, not a meaningful relationship there, scarcely a one-night stand. Cynthia, whose name he was forgetting even when he was with her, represented more than he wished for, however. He had been with his first woman since Joanna. He could accomplish this with more grace next time, more affection, do it better – but it would be with someone else, not with Joanna, never again with Joanna. He had been holding himself off from accepting this, and now he had crossed over. His wife had left him, and if your wife leaves you, somewhere along the line you have to begin to deal with other women. He was right back in the singles' scene.

If he had been seduced into believing that all he had to do was show up at a party and end up in bed with someone, he would learn otherwise at the next week-end's cocktail party where no one was enthralled with him, and the week-end after that, and the Labor Day week-end when everybody scrambled around to make connections, and he stood out in the walk at twilight with a drink in his hand watching people on their way to house parties, stopping the most elegant-looking person he had seen in weeks, a pretty girl in a white dress. He complimented her on how pretty she was and she smiled and did not seem at all uninterested, but she was on her way to this party and he could not go. He watched her leave, not to meet up with her again because he had a four-year-old boy in the house who had just thrown up on the living-room floor and was resting in his room, and his daddy could not leave him to chase phantom ladies in white. Watching people on their way to the summer's last parties, he envied them for how simple it was to be on their own, with only themselves to worry about, while he could not even stroll down the walk.

'How are you doing, pussycat?'

'I'm sick, Daddy.'

'I know. I think you ate too much popcorn at Joey's house.'

'I ate too much popcorn at Joey's house.'

'Try to sleep now, honey. Tomorrow is our last day here. We'll have a good time. We'll build the biggest sandcastle of the summer.'

'I don't want to go home.'

'Well, it's going to be the fall. The fall is terrific in New York. So go to sleep now.'

'Sit here, Daddy, until I fall asleep.'

'Okay, pussycat.'

'I ate too much popcorn at Joey's house.'

On the last day at Chez Gloria, Ellen, the editor, who had not really met one person all summer, could not get out of her chair. George, the psychiatrist, Johnny-on-the-spot with his analysis, said Ellen was a highly suggestible person and was negatively influenced by the event of the July Fourth week-end when her former housemate also could not get out of her chair. It became part of the Fire Island folklore, going into the aural history of the island, a record, like most doubles by a shortstop in a single season – most nervous breakdowns in a group house in a single season.

It was a grubby game Ted was going to be making his come-back in, and it may have been over in Fire Island, but he knew by now that it was going to be a very long season.

CHAPTER NINE

The divorce took seven minutes. The judge held the hearing in his chambers. John Shaunessy, the lawyer and football buff, sent his team up the middle, a few affidavits, the wife was not contesting, a doctor's letter saying the husband had been tense, Ted answered a printed series of questions, he said the experience had been upsetting, and the judge did not appear to be involved. They rolled over the opposition, who did not put a team on the field. Judgment granted on the divorce and custody on the grounds of 'cruel and inhuman treatment rendering co-habitation unsafe or improper.' Ten days later the actual papers signed by the judge came by mail, and Ted Kramer and Joanna Kramer were legally divorced.

Ted felt a gesture was in order. He took Billy out to Burger King. The celebration was restrained, since all Billy was celebrating was a large order for French fries. The boy had a fragile enough hold on what marriage was and where babies came from, so Ted had elected not to complicate his life by discussing pending judicial proceedings. Now he wanted him to know.

'Billy, there's something called divorce. It's when two people who were married get un-married.'

'I know. Seth got divorced.'

'Seth's parents got divorced. Like your mommy and daddy. Your mommy and daddy are divorced now, Billy.'

'Didn't Mommy say she'd send me presents?'

I don't speak for the lady, Billy.

'Maybe she will.'

Ted looked at him as if he were admiring a painting, Billy in his Burger King crown.

'Can I have some more French fries?'

'No, wise guy, you had enough.'

This was pleasant enough, but eating junk food with his son did not seem appropriate to the event, which had a $2000 price tag on it. He thought he owed himself more. At the restaurant he called a teenager in his building who had offered her baby-sitting services and he arranged for her to sit that evening. There was not a woman in his life to celebrate this with him. In the two months since Fire Island he had let his social life, if it could have been called that, go untended. Larry would have been too manic. He did not want to go by himself to a bar and tell a stranger his life's story. He called dentist Charlie.

Charlie had moved into a studio apartment with his hygienist, but they broke up after only two weeks of exclusivity. Charlie called Ted then, and said the guys should stick together and see each other. When Ted asked about getting together that very night, Charlie was ecstatic. They met on Second Avenue and 72nd Street in the heart of the singles' bars. The plan was to drink their way along the line. Ted was wearing a corduroy jacket, sweater and slacks. Charlie, a portly man of forty-five, appeared in a blazer, and with plaid pants so loud they were like Op Art.

The first place they chose was called Pals, a suitable-looking bar from the outside. When they walked in, it was all men, dressed in leather. A cowboy at the door with a bulging crotch and leather eyes, said, 'Hi tigers,' and they scampered out of the corral. Rio Rita's was next, with a blaring jukebox and a scene at the bar that looked like a

Fire Island deck. College kids, Ted decided, and over a couple of drinks, he listened to Charlie absolve him of the blame for the break-up with Thelma. Hansel's had so many strapping lads and lassies Ted wondered if they had stumbled into a European youth festival. Ted learned there that Thelma was going out with a colleague of Charlie's, another dentist. By the time they reached Zapata's, the crowd was getting older, but with Ted and Charlie still the oldest in sight. There, Charlie absolved Ted of the blame for his break-up with his dental hygienist. Ted, blurry from vodka, was not certain if he had been involved. At Glitter, the crowd was so sophisticated and the place so crowded, these two non-regulars were not permitted to stand at the bar, so they began to weave down the street and landed on bar stools in Home Again.

'We have said a total of sixteen dumb things to women at the various bars thus far,' Ted remarked, more aware of the inanity of saying anything better than dumb at a bar than Charlie, who was stuck like a broken record on 'Hi, little girl. What's *your* name?' Charlie approached a pretty girl looking up-to-the-second chic in a boy scout uniform and he tried out his line. The boy scout walked away to start a fire elsewhere.

Ted and Charlie leaned against a wall on Second Avenue and had the heart-to-heart they were building to all night, except they were too smashed to have it. 'Did I ever tell you how sorry I was about Joanna?' Charlie said. Ted said, 'I try not to think of her.' Charlie said, 'I think of Thelma all the time,' and Charlie started to cry. Ted helped him along the street and suggested, with the clarity of a drunk, that they have a nightcap in The Emerald Isle, rye and soda, 85¢ special. Charlie tried to fall asleep, Ted dragged him out of the bar, walked him home, and then, attempting to draw himself up so that his new teenage baby-sitter would think he was a perfect gentleman, Ted entered the house and thanked her for a lovely evening.

He had informed some of the people around him about the divorce. He thought he should inform Joanna. When his lawyer began legal proceedings, Ted obtained an address from Joanna's parents, a post office box number in La Jolla, California. He was going to send her a copy of the papers. Diplomatic relations had not improved between Ted and Joanna's parents. They came into New York again and did not have much to say to *him*. 'Ask him what time we should bring the boy home,' her father said. Ted wanted to know if they had heard from Joanna and her mother told him, 'If Joanna wishes to inform you as to her activities, she is of age to do so.' Ted noticed that some hostility seemed to be directed at Joanna, and he concluded they might not know themselves of Joanna's activities. Thelma, his expert on psychology, having been in analysis for seven years, said Joanna could be rebelling against her parents also, and that they might not know very much about what Joanna was doing. Joanna, originally, left it for Ted to tell them, running out on her parents, too, she surmised.

'You should worry about your own psyche, though,' Thelma said.

'Right. The hell with her.'

'That's not what I mean. I really think you should go into therapy. This whole thing has happened to you. Don't you want to know why?'

'Ask Joanna.'

'You're part of it, Ted. Why don't you see my doctor?'

'I don't think so. It's too late for that.'

He sat with the legal papers in front of him, composing notes in his mind to Joanna. 'You're free to get married in Nevada or New York, baby.' No, too childish. 'I thought while sending you this I would tell you how we've been doing, specifically, how Billy has been doing.' No, she hadn't asked. He decided to put it in an envelope, send it without a note and let it speak for itself. They had communicated in their times together by eyes, by touch, by words, and now they communicated by divorce decree.

Ted's parents arrived in New York on a long-promised visit, two rotund figures with suntans.

'The boy is so thin,' his mother said.

'He's fine. That's the way he's built.'

'I know a thin child. I wasn't in the restaurant business for nothing.'

After deciding 'this Polish one' was not feeding him properly – they had met Etta when they arrived and greeted her with a warmth reserved for delivery boys – Dora Kramer decided to embark on her own grandparents' festival, filling the refrigerator with roasts and chickens which she cooked and which Billy would not eat.

'I don't understand his eating habits.'

'Try pizza,' Ted said.

'Billy, don't you like your grandma's pot roast?' attempting guilt on him.

'No, Grandma. It's hard to chew.'

Ted wanted to embrace him right there. Generations had tolerated Dora Kramer's overcooking, and only William Kramer, his boy, had stood up to her. Billy said good night, after not playing with a complicated jigsaw puzzle his grandparents had brought which would have tested a ten-year-old.

'Don't you like the nice puzzle Grandma picked out for you?'

'No, Grandma. The pieces are too tiny.'

Afterwards, the grown-ups were able to talk freely, Dora getting to her more serious concerns.

'She's not much of a cleaner, this Etta.'

'She does okay. We're making out all right here.'

She declined to answer. Whether they came down from Boston or up from Florida, her parents or his, they were unified in their thinking in not finding him competent. He would not accept their appraisal.

'Billy is a fabulous child, Mother.'

'He has a faraway look in his eyes.'

'I think he's been pretty happy, considering.'

'What do you think, Harold?' she asked.

'Yeah, he's too thin,' he said.

When they were ready to leave, Dora took a final look at the apartment.

'You should fix this place up.'

'What's wrong with it?' Ted said.

'It's *her* place. I'm surprised you didn't get rid of some of this stuff.'

The apartment had been furnished in a modern, eclectic style – beiges and browns, a Swedish couch, Indian print curtains in the living-room, a butcher block dining-room table in the dining alcove – tasteful, but not specifically Ted's taste, which was undefined. These were largely Joanna's decorating decisions. After she left, he just never thought to change it.

'And this thing.' It was a large, black ceramic ashtray, a gift from Joanna's parents. 'What are you still doing with it?'

'Thank you for coming,' he said.

When they were gone, Ted had a headache. Was his mother dead centre on the apartment? Was he so passive that he just accepted his state, did not change what he should have? Should he have redecorated the apartment, *her* apartment? Wouldn't that have upset Billy? Wasn't he using Billy, if he thought that it would have upset him? He took the ashtray which nobody liked, not even Joanna, and threw it down the incinerator. Was there something basically wrong with him that he had not done it earlier? He was not sure.

After Larry, seemingly uncomplicated Larry, confided that he had gone into analysis, Ted began to acknowledge darker forces out there, or in there.

'I'm afraid of a Casanova complex, old buddy. I make it with a lot of ladies because I'm afraid that I'm a fag.'

'Larry, are you kidding?'

'I'm not saying I'm a fag. I'm not saying that I've got a Casanova complex. I'm saying that I'm afraid I've got one and that's what we're working on.'

'It's pretty complicated.'

'I know. Heavy shit. But I love it.'

Three weeks more passed, with the biggest event on Ted's fall social calendar a Saturday matinee of *Aladdin* with Billy. Even Charlie had become a mover, passing him phone numbers, while he was still home at night, bringing work home from the office. Two more uncalled numbers went into a file. What about all the people who seemed to have been helped by therapy? He decided to call Thelma for the number of her doctor.

Her therapist said he would be available for a consultation at a fee of $40. Justifying it on the grounds that if he spent $55 on one of Billy's recent head colds, he could spend $40 for his mental health, he made an appointment. Dr Martin Graham was in his forties. He wore a bright Italian silk sports shirt open at the neck,

'Where have you gone, Sigmund Freud?' Ted said.

'Meaning?'

'I expected a bearded man in a heavy suit.'

'Relax, Mr Kramer.'

They sat opposite one another across the doctor's desk. Ted attempted to be composed – There's nothing wrong with me, Doctor – as he told him about his marriage, Joanna's leaving, and the events of the past few months. The doctor listened carefully, asked him a few questions – how he felt about some of the situations, and did not take any notes, Ted wondering if he had failed to say anything noteworthy.

'Okay. Mr Kramer, a consultation is really just an exploration. One of the things that's wrong with it, and what I object to, is you get into a kind of instant analysis.'

'Like you've got a such-and-so complex,' Ted said nervously.

'Something like that. So let me just give you some impressions. They may be off the wall, they may be on target. I don't know.'

Ted thought it should be a science by now and not an I-don't-know.

'Your feelings about all this seem to be pushed way down. Like where is your anger? You talked about not going out. Okay. Are you angry at women now? Your mother? Your father? Whatever you had at home there doesn't sound like *The Waltons*.'

Ted smiled, but he did not feel like smiling.

'It's possible – and again, this is just an impression – that you've got a history from your family experiences of pushing down your feelings, and that could have seeped into your marriage, and it could be holding you back now.'

'You're saying I should be in therapy.'

'We get all kinds, Mr Kramer. Some people can't function. Some people have a specific, overriding problem and you give them first-aid. Some people could just use help, generally, to understand where they're coming from.'

'Me?'

'I'm not selling you. It's for you to decide. I think you could be helped by therapy. I don't think you're without problems, Mr Kramer.'

He told Ted he charged $40 an hour, and assuming one of his patients went through with his plans to terminate, he could take Ted on. Two or three times a week would be best, the doctor thought, one would be the absolute minimum. He did not see it as first-aid, and Ted knew that people often stayed in therapy for years. It was a great deal of money to Ted and the doctor agreed, but he did not know of anyone he could recommend who charged less. There was group therapy – he did not feel it was helpful enough without regular therapy included. There were clinics, if they would take him, with less experienced therapists, but they were also moving up with their rates. Ted had to make the decision about how much it was worth to have a clearer view of himself and to feel better about himself, as the doctor phrased it.

'I am getting by, though. I mean, for the most part, I do have things pretty well together,' going back to his there's-nothing-wrong-with-me-doctor stance. The doctor was the doctor.

'Are you looking for me to give you a little star, Mr Kramer? Just to be getting by is not necessarily everything.'

The time was up and they shook hands.

'Doctor, so long as I'm here, could I ask you a couple of quick questions?'

'If I can answer them.'

'In your opinion' – he felt foolish asking, but he went on

with it – 'do you think I should have redecorated my apartment?'

The doctor did not laugh at him. He took the question seriously.

'Are you unhappy with the way it looks?'

'No.'

'Then why would you want to change it?'

'Right.'

He had a last question.

'Do you think I should go out more?' and this time Ted laughed, trying to immediately downgrade his asking.

'Do you want to go out more?' he said, again taking it seriously.

'Yes, I do.'

'Then go.'

Ted pondered the idea of analysis for himself. He liked the man's style and his lack of jargon. Maybe this person could help him. But he had no idea of how he could possibly afford $40 a week to go into therapy, or even at bargain rates, $30 on a week-in, week-out basis. Not with the cost of a housekeeper and real medical bills. What was rattling around inside him would have to go unsorted, he decided. He would settle for getting by. He would leave the apartment as is. And he would go out more. He would definitely go out more. Doctor's orders.

CHAPTER TEN

Ted Kramer found the social landscape altered since he had first passed this way. For some of the women, marriage was 'obsolete,' as Tania, a dancer in her twenties told him. She was also 'into women,' she informed him in bed. 'But don't let it throw you. You're a nice guy. I dig it with you, too.'

Many of the women were divorced now, the first marriages had had sufficient time to break down under wear. A few of the women, in a non-competitiveness he could not recall, would give him names of their friends to phone when it was apparent that A Great Love was not on the premises. If the woman also had a child at home, a simple evening could take on the urgency of *Beat the Clock*. The meter was running on both sides. He was paying for a sitter, she was paying for a sitter. At $2 an hour each, it would cost them $4 an hour, total, just to sit there. Something big had to happen fast. They either had to like each other fast or decide that they were going to bed with each other fast. And bed did not just mean bed. It meant more time on the clock, more money for sitters, possible taxicabs, possible taxicabs for sitters. If they were at a midpoint geographically in the city and went back to his house, he would have to release his sitter, and therefore be unavailable to take the woman home, so she would have to take a cab. If he offered to pay for the woman's cab, it brought up the question of her taking money from him. She had to figure out if she wanted to pay extra for *her* sitter, as well as pay for her own cab. At this point, the players might be having trouble following the game out of sheer exhaustion, since they were both parents and were likely up earlier in the morning than most civilians.

The logistics could begin to take precedence over the experience. This happened to Ted one evening when he was saying to himself, it's 10:30, $6 in sitting. Do we stay or do we make love? If we make love, I think we should go in the next five minutes or it's another hour in sitting, and he was short of cash that week. So he had turned his attention from her to watch the clock, none of this having anything at all to do with making love. On some nights, he was not aware of the meter running – the person, the warmth between them became dominant – but not very often.

Billy had little stake in his father's social life.

'Are you going out again, Daddy?'

'I have friends like you have friends. You see your friends in the day and I see my friends at night.'

'I'm going to miss you.'

'I'll miss *you*. But I'll see you in the morning.'

'Don't go out, Daddy, please.'

'I have to.'

In school, Billy had begun grabbing toys from other children, as though to hold on to as much around him as he could. Ted spoke to the pediatrician and to the nursery school teachers, and they thought it was a reaction to Joanna's absence, and could pass or not. The times Ted spent with Billy were tranquil for the most part, except when Ted's fatigue became entwined with Billy's need to be clingy and Ted, feeling choked, had to physically pull him off his arm or his leg, hating to do it, but unable to bear his pulling at him like that.

Ted met a woman lawyer at a party. Phyllis was from Cleveland, in her late twenties, an intense woman. She wore bulky tweed clothing, a few degrees out of fashion. She was extremely literal, the conversations between them were high-level and serious. They were having dinner at a restaurant, and he was not watching the clock this night. They decided to go back for, euphemistically, 'coffee' at his place.

In the night, getting ready to leave, she went out in the hall towards the bathroom. Billy, very quietly, had also been up and was coming *out* of the bathroom. They stopped and stared at each other in the darkness, like two startled deer, she, naked, Billy in his giraffe pyjamas, holding his people.

'Who are you?' he said.

'Phyllis. I'm a friend of your father's,' she said, wanting to be specific.

He stared intently at her and she attempted to cover herself, assuming it was inappropriate to do otherwise in front of a child. They were fixed in place. He kept staring at her in the dark. There was obviously something of great importance on his mind.

'Do you like fried chicken?' he said.

'Yes,' she replied.

Satisfied with the exchange, he walked into his room and went to sleep.

'I just met your son.'

'Oh?'

'He wanted to know if I liked fried chicken.'

Ted began to laugh. 'Do you?'

'Yes, I like fried chicken. This is quite a bit to handle.'

'It is?'

'This is not a conventional situation,' she said rather literally.

Phyllis stayed in his life for two months. She was impatient with small talk, they discussed social issues, the nation's morality. Ted read so many magazines, he was able to be up-to-the-week on current thinking. They had evolved to an intellectual relationship with sex. Her congressman from Cleveland offered her a job in Washington. She thought the position was desirable and that it was too early in their relationship to jeopardize 'an important career decision,' she said, and Ted, ambivalent about his own feelings about her, agreed. 'Also, to be honest,' she told him, 'I don't think I am prepared for such an ambitious undertaking as this.' They said goodbye, kissing warmly, and promised to write or call, and neither of them did.

Ted satisfied himself that he had been able to break out of the one-night, two-night carrousel he had been on. Someone had been in his life for a couple of months. But Phyllis had pointed out to him that it could be awkward for a woman to walk into 'such an ambitious undertaking as this,' with a divorced man and a little boy.

Ted and Thelma became close friends. He did not have much confidence in his romantic interludes and he thought if he tried to make love to Thelma, he might gain a night and lose a friend. They both set aside ideas of becoming involved on any other level than friendship, and were there for each other, to support each other, to help each other get free for a few hours. If Ted worried, as he had begun to, that he was focused too much on the child, it was Thelma who reminded him this was inevitable – they were parents alone with their children, and Billy was an only child. As an assembled family group, they went to the playground one day, and it was a particularly difficult time. The children spent the day scrapping. 'I don't like Kim. She's bossy.' 'I don't like Billy. He's rough.' They argued over sand toys, apple juice, motorcycles, Ted and Thelma spending the afternoon as peacemakers. Ted took a sobbing Billy to the other side of the playground to calm him down. As he was walking across the playground, coming in the other direction was a father with his small boy.

'If you walk them out,' the man volunteered, 'and take them out to the furthest ices stand, and they eat the ices there, and you walk them back, it'll kill twenty minutes.'

Ted could not understand what the man was saying to him.

'Twenty minutes, easy, I'm telling you.'

The man was a Sunday father, putting in his time, or his wife was off shopping somewhere and would be back soon.

'I've got a little more than twenty minutes to kill,' Ted said.

The day concluded with Billy and Kim eventually joining forces to throw sand at a third boy, whose mother started screaming at Thelma, calling her 'an animal.' Billy was keyed up so high, it took a hot bath and many stories to get him to sleep. Ted wondered if he had been acting up that day or just being boisterous. Kim was capable of sitting for much longer periods, painting or colouring, than Billy, who was more random in his attention. Was it because boys and girls were different, or was it because these two particular children were different? Was it because he was hyperactive? Is he all right? *Am* I watching him too closely? God, I love him. Jesus, what a shitty day!

Broken pieces from plastic trucks, wooden people with splintered torsos, loose pages out of torn colouring books – Billy's room was littered with unusable items and Ted, the Grim Reaper, was coming through on a clean-up, Billy following him, fighting over every stubby Crayola.

'By the time you're ten, this place will look like the Collier Brothers lived in it.'

'Who?'

'Two old men and they had a room that looked like yours.'

He had been tempted to do this at a time when Billy was out, but months later Billy would be upset to discover a missing broken car.

'Out!' A wind-up truck that no longer wound up.

'No. I love that.'

Ted surveyed the room. It was still Collier Brothers. He decided to do it a different way. He took Billy to a hardware store and bought several clear plastic boxes. Somehow it came to $14 just to organize part of a child's room.

'Now, try to keep all the crayons in the crayon box and all the little cars in the little-car box.'

'Daddy, if I'm using the crayons, the box will be empty. How will I know it's the crayon box?'

They were into Zen crayons.

'I'll put labels on the boxes.'

'I can't read.'

Ted could not resist laughing.

'Why are you laughing?'

'I'm sorry. You're right. It isn't funny. You will read one day. Until then, I'll tape one of whatever is supposed to be inside the box, outside the box, and then you'll know what's supposed to be inside the box. Did you follow that?'

'Oh, sure. Good idea.'

'You're the top pussycat, pussycat.'

On the floor, on his knees, combining three different sets of crayons into the crayon box, he had an insight, like an apple or a Crayola that landed on his head. Clean it up! Combine!

The next morning he was waiting outside Jim O'Connor's office with his idea.

The company he worked for published a magazine in each of several leisure areas – photography, skiing, boating, tennis, and travel. It had suddenly occurred to Ted that they could combine all of their magazines into one package. This would be an across-the-board buy for advertisers at a special rate.

'It's so logical. We could still go on selling each book just as we've been doing. Except we'd have this new package on the side.'

'With a name.'

'We could call it anything we want. The Leisure Package.'

'Ted, I'd like to tell you it's brilliant, but it's not.'

'I thought it was.'

'What it is – is perfect. Perfect! What the hell have we been doing here? Why didn't anybody think of it? Perfect, but not brilliant.'

'I'll take a perfect.'

He had never seen Jim O'Connor respond to an idea with such enthusiasm, which O'Connor carried on to the research department, which was put to work that morning on statistics, and to the promotion department, which was to come up with a campaign immediately for The Leisure Package. Within a week, a sales presentation had been prepared for Ted to use on exploratory sales calls for the company's new advertising package, within two weeks a rate card and promotional brochure had been distributed to their sales list, and within three weeks ads began appearing in the advertising trade press selling The Leisure Package. A company that had been struggling along was now using this new sales concept as a sign of vitality. The response at advertising agencies was positive. Ted was taken off the travel magazine he worked on to do the selling of the new concept. He was receiving promises of revised advertising schedules and in several cases, orders for ads. The publisher and owner of the company, a dapper little man named Mo Fisher, who was seen as a presence moving in and out of the office with golf clubs and $400 suits stopped Ted in the hall. His last words to Ted had been several years before when Ted first joined the company. He said, 'Good to have you aboard,' and had not spoken to him since. 'Nice going,' he said, and kept on walking to the golf course.

In the late fall in New York, the city was lovely – cool, clear weather, people promenading, the trees in the parks were doing their best to be autumnal. On Saturdays and Sundays Ted took long bicycle rides with Billy behind him in the seat through Central Park, stopping off at the zoo and at playgrounds. Billy was four and a half and had grown out of a baby-clothes look and was now wearing authentic little big-boy pants, jerseys with football numbers, a ski jacket and ski hat. With his dark saucer eyes and small nose, and now in his big-boy clothes, Ted thought him to be the most beautiful child he had ever seen. Ted had his successes at work during the week, and on the week-ends he was with Billy for their autumn days out-doors, the city becoming the setting for this love affair of a father with his little boy.

The new advertising campaign was working. At a time when two of the other salesmen were told to look for pink slips for Christmas, Ted was promised a $1500 bonus. On one of his sales calls to a new agency on his list, he met a secretary, a gamine wearing dungarees and a sweat shirt. She was twenty years old and he had not gone out with anyone that young virtually since he was twenty years old. She lived in a studio apartment in a walk-up in Greenwich Village and he was faintly surprised to discover anyone still did that. Angelica Coleman. She walked through his life with sandals and insouciance. Going out with an older man who had a child was 'experiential.' The experience was 'spacey.' She was going to 'get my act together' in New York and 'do the business thing,' and why didn't he want to smoke dope?

'I can't. I mean, I used to, now and then. But I can't now.'

'Why not?'

'Well, what if I have a bad experience? I've got to stay intact. I've got a kid at home.'

'Profound.'

On a rainy Sunday, she stopped at Ted's apartment without calling, wheeling in her ten-speed bicycle, and got down on the floor with Billy and played with him for an hour. He had never seen anyone relate to Billy so openly. With her wet hair, and wearing one of Ted's sweat shirts, she looked even younger than usual. He was in a time machine. He was dating a camp counsellor from the girls' side of Camp Tamarac who had come over for rainy-day-play in his bunk.

After a few weeks, he decided they did not have enough in common 'experientially.' It was a long way from the lyrics of Oscar Hammerstein to David Bowie.

He phoned to tell her.

'Angie, I'm just too old for you.'

'You're not *that* old.'

'I'll be forty.'

'Forty. Wow!'

Ted received his bonus at work and to celebrate he made a reservation at Jorgés, a new, expensive restaurant. He walked in with Billy of the combined crayons.

'Are *you* the two for Kramer?' the maître d' said disdainfully.

'We are.'

'We don't have a high chair.'

'I don't sit in a high chair,' Billy protested on behalf of himself.

The maître d' led them to a not very desirable table near the kitchen, turning them over to an equally disdainful waiter. Ted ordered a vodka martini and a ginger ale for Billy. Another waiter passed by en route to a table with a giant broiled lobster.

'What's that?' Billy asked, apprehensively.

'Lobster.'

'I don't want it.'

'You don't have to have it.'

'Lobster from the water?'

'Yes.'

'People eat it?'

This was a difficult issue, the origin of food. That lamb chops came from little lambs, and hamburgers from animals that looked like Bessie the Cow, and if a child got on that track, who could predict when he might eat again? Ted recited suitable items on the menu – steak, lamb chops – and on the beat, Billy wanted to know where they came from and immediately lost his appetite.

'I'll have a sirloin, rare. And a grilled-cheese sandwich.'

'No grilled cheese, sir,' the waiter said in a typical I'm-an-actor-I-don't-have-to-do-this-for-a-living New York waiter voice.

'Tell the chef. I don't care what it costs. Make one.'

The maître d' appeared.

'Sir, this is not a diner.'

'The child is a vegetarian.'

'Then let him eat vegetables.'

'He doesn't eat vegetables.'

'Then how can he be a vegetarian?'

'He doesn't have to be. He's four and a half.'

To quieten the lunatic and keep order in his restaurant, the maître d' saw that the order was forthcoming. At the table, they chatted about nursery school events, Billy enjoyed watching grownups eat, and they savoured the celebration dinner, Billy in a special-for-the-occasion shirt and tie, sitting on his knees, the only person of his height on the premises.

As they were leaving, Ted, delighted with the meal, turned to the maître d', who had nearly fainted at the sight of the chocolate ice-cream Billy had for dessert making its way off Billy's chin on to the white tablecloth.

'You shouldn't be so rude to royalty,' Ted said, his arm around Billy, proudly leading his boy out.

'Really?' the maître d' said, momentarily uncertain.

'He's the Infant King of Spain.'

CHAPTER ELEVEN

'Merry Christmas, Ted. It's Joanna.'

'Joanna?'

'I'm coming to New York. I'm on my way through to visit my parents. I want to see Billy.'

She spoke quickly in a flat tone.

'How are you?' he said, completely off-stride.

'I'm fine,' brushing his question aside. 'I want to see him. I'll be in New York Saturday. I'd rather not come to the apartment if it's all the same to you.'

In her tone of voice and choice of words, she was making it clear. This was not a phone call of reconciliation.

'You want to see Billy?'

'I'll be at the Americana. Can you bring him there at ten

a.m., Saturday? I'll spend the day with him, take him around, sight-see. I'll have him back by his bedtime.'

'I don't know.'

'Why? Are you going to be away?'

'No. I just don't know.'

'You don't know what?'

'It could be disruptive.'

'Come on, Ted. I'm not the Wicked Witch of the West. I'm the boy's mother. I want to see him.'

'I really have to think about it.'

'Ted, don't be a shmuck.'

'Oh, that's persuasive.'

'I didn't mean that. Please, Ted. Let me see him.'

'I'll have to sleep on it.'

'I'll call you tomorrow.'

He had a consultation with Thelma, who confirmed what did not require much confirmation for Ted – that Joanna obviously was not seeking to return to his arms. As to the wisdom of her seeing Billy, Thelma was thinking more of Joanna. 'The price of independence,' she said. 'It must be rough.'

Ted attempted to clarify his thoughts by placing his exact position. He called the lawyer.

'Do you think she'll kidnap him?' Shaunessy asked.

'I wasn't thinking of that.'

'It's been done.'

'I don't know what's on her mind. I doubt kidnapping.'

'Well, you're within your legal rights to oppose her on seeing the kid. And she's within her rights to get a court order to see him. A judge would grant it. Mother, Christmas. You'd never win. On a practical basis, I'd say if you don't think there's a risk of a kidnap, you'd save yourself a lot of hassle to just give her the day with him.'

Was it better for Billy to see his mother or better for him not to? Should he force her to go to court and make her work for it? If he did, he would be harassing her at the expense of stirring up his insides. Would she possibly kidnap him? When Joanna called, he put the question directly to her.

D

'You wouldn't be thinking of kidnapping him, would you?'

'What? Ted, you can stay twenty paces behind all day, if you want to. You can sneak around corners and tail me. I'm coming into New York for a few lousy hours, I'm going on to Boston, and then I'm going back to California. And that's the whole deal. I just want to go to F.A.O. Schwarz at Christmas with my son and buy him a goddamn toy! What do I have to do, beg?'

'Okay, Joanna. Saturday, the Americana at ten.'

Ted informed Billy that his mommy was coming to New York and was going to spend Saturday with him.

'My mommy?'

'Yes, Billy.'

The child grew pensive.

'Maybe she'll buy me something,' he said.

Ted took extra care with Billy that morning, brushed his hair, dressed him in his best shirt and pants, and made certain he, too, was wearing his best – no frayed edges here. They arrived at the Americana, and promptly at ten, Joanna emerged from the elevator. Ted felt weak. She looked stunning. She was wearing a white coat, a bright scarf on her head and had an attractive mid-winter tan. The girls at parties, the gamines in sweat shirts, all his carrousel riders were also-rans against her.

Joanna did not look at Ted. She went straight for Billy, kneeling in front of him. 'Oh, Billy.' She hugged him to her, cradling his head beneath her chin, and she started to cry. Then she stood up to appraise him.

'Hello, Billy boy.'

'Hello, Mommy.'

For the first time, she turned to Ted.

'Thank you. I'll see you here at six.'

Ted just nodded.

'Come,' she said. 'We'll have a nice day,' and she took Billy by the hand and led him out of the hotel lobby.

Ted was anxious all day. If she kept her word and after seeing the boy left immediately for points elsewhere, would this be jarring to Billy – would he feel lifted up and then dropped again? What right had she to make such an invasion?

Every legal right, he conceded. On edge, he went to a double feature, window shopped, and was back in the hotel lobby forty minutes early, waiting.

Joanna returned with Billy a few minutes before six. The boy looked tired from a long day, but was smiling.

'Look, Daddy,' he said, holding up a box of plastic figures. 'Weebles wobble but they don't fall down.'

'Weebles.'

'My mommy bought them for me.'

Joanna took a last look at Billy and then closed her eyes, as if the sight of him were too dazzling for her.

'See you, Billy,' she said, hugging him. 'Ge a good boy now.'

'See you, Mommy. Thank you for the weebles.'

She turned and, without looking back, went into the elevator.

So Joanna Kramer had not come East to kidnap her child, or reconcile with Ted, or stay. She was passing through. She was there to see her parents and spend a day with Billy. Ted learned later from her parents that Joanna visited with them for a day in Boston and then, just as she said she was going to do, she went back to California. Apparently, Joanna could not imagine coming all that distance without seeing the boy, but the distance she would have had to travel to do anything more than that was too far.

The boy survived the day without a sign of disturbance, relying on a child's facility to accept the world as it appears to him. Mommy was here. Mommy was gone. The sky is blue. People eat lobsters. Mommy was gone. Daddy was here. He got weebles. Weebles wobble and they don't fall down.

'Did you have a nice time?' Ted asked, probing.

'Yes, it was nice.'

Do you miss Mommy, too? But this Ted did not ask.

Ted Kramer resented his former wife's intrusion into his organizational structure, and his emotions. Seeing her again was unnerving. Once, he was married to the prettiest girl at the party and somehow she got away, and now the party was dull. 'Serial relationships' was Thelma's term for the style of their social lives, one person after another, nothing, no one sustained. Ted's two months with Phyllis, the lawyer, had exceeded any of his friends' totals. Thelma said they were all bruised people, Charlie insisted it was the time of his life now, and Larry was still compacting entire relationships into a week-end.

Ted might find himself in the playground on a Saturday rocking Billy in a swing alongside Thelma rocking Kim, and on the following day alongside Charlie rocking Kim. Charlie and Thelma's divorce was final, Ted having attended successive, joyless divorce celebration dinners at each of their apartments.

'Think you'll ever get married again?' Charlie asked, as the two men shivered in a patch of sun in the playground, watching their children playing in the snow.

'Beats me. With a child already, I'm what they call in advertising a hard sell.'

'I was thinking . . . what if I get married again and what if I have another kid, and get divorced again and have to pay child support twice?'

'Charlie, all those what-ifs. I don't think you can set that up as a reason not to.'

'I know. But the money! That's a lot of cavities.'

Thelma had her own perspective on re-marriage. She aired it in a guerrilla conversation, a few adult remarks stolen from the children's hour as, from the phonograph in Billy's bedroom, Oscar the Grouch shouted how he loved trash, and the children played hide-and-seek through the house.

'The first time you marry for love, but of course, you get divorced. The second time, you know that love was invented by Hallmark. So you marry for other things.'

'Hold it,' he said. 'Billy and Kim! Turn down Oscar or turn down yourselves!'

'So . . . the second marriage is really to confirm your own life style or your own views. You know, the first time, you marry your mother.'

'I didn't know that, Thelma. I don't think you should let that get around.'

'But the second time, you marry yourself.'

'You just saved me a lot of trouble. Then I'm already married.'

It was Larry who broke away from the pack after years of running. He was marrying Ellen Fried, a twenty-nine-year-old teacher in the city public schools system. Larry had met her on Fire Island and had been seeing her while dating other women, as was his style. Now he had decided to retire his girlmobile. Ted had met Ellen several times and noticed she was a calming influence on Larry. She was soft-spoken, thoughtful, plainer and more dignified than Larry's usual women.

The wedding was held in a small suite at the Plaza Hotel, a few friends and the immediate families, which in this case included Larry's children from his first marriage, a girl of fourteen and a boy of sixteen. Ted remembered them when they were babies. It all goes so fast, he thought.

In a park-bench conversation he had overheard a woman saying to Thelma, 'None of it matters. They don't remember much of anything from before the age of five.' Ted had disagreed, not wanting to think any of his caring would be nullified. The woman claimed she heard a discussion of it on television. 'They have sense memories. Specifically, they don't remember. Maybe nothing that happens to your child today will he remember.' It was a day Billy had been bopped on the head with a metal truck by another child. 'He's lucky, then,' Ted said. This was worth a chuckle, at the time. Now he wondered how much Billy would retain. And later on, when he was older, when he reached the age of Larry's children, and moved beyond, what kind of impact would he have made on his son?

'Billy, do you know what Daddy does for a living?'

'You have a job.'

'Yes, but do you know what kind of job?'

'In an office.'

'That's right. You've seen ads in magazines. Well, I get the companies to put the ads in the magazines.'

Suddenly, it had become very important to Ted to fix his place for his son.

'Would you like to see my office? Would you like to see where I work?'

'Sure.'

'I want you to.'

On a Saturday, Ted took Billy to his office building on Madison Avenue and 57th Street. A uniformed guard was in the lobby, and Billy seemed afraid until Ted showed a card and got them through. A few points for big Daddy who was not afraid. The company's offices were locked, and Ted opened the outside door with a key and turned on the lights. The long corridors were cavernous to a child. Ted led him to his office.

'See? That's my name.'

'That's my name, too. Kramer.'

He unlocked the door and took Billy inside. The office was on the fourteenth floor, and from Ted's window he had a view east and west on 57th Street.

'Oh, Daddy, it's so high. It's beautiful,' and he pressed his face against the window.

He sat down in his father's chair and swung himself around.

'I like your office, Daddy.'

'Thank you, pal. My pal.'

Billy had run through all the right little-boy-looking-up-to-his-father reactions as far as Ted was concerned. Billy *was* his pal. He had been a constant for Ted throughout these months. So he might not remember everything about his father from these times. He might not even care, painful as that might be for Ted. But they had been living through a loss together. They were allies.

I will always be there for you, my Billy. Always.

'There's something I don't like here, Daddy. I don't like the pictures.'

The office was decorated with magazine covers from the company's early days.

'You should have zebras.'

'Why don't you draw me some and I'll put them up?'

The child drew some misshapen creatures with stripes

and his father put them up.

Joanna's parents arrived from Boston. The tinge of anger towards Joanna he had detected their last time in New York seemed to have settled into sadness.

'This is really something,' Harriet said to him when Billy was out of the room. 'The grandparents see more of the child than the mother.'

Ted guessed that they hoped Joanna would have stayed when she came through and not have returned so abruptly to California, as he now learned she had done.

'What does she do there? For a living, I mean?'

'You don't know?'

'I don't know anything about her life, Harriet. Nothing at all.'

'She works for Hertz. She's one of those girls who smiles and rents you a car.'

'Really?.'

'She left her family, her child, to go to California to rent cars,' Harriet said.

Ted brushed quickly over the lack of status Harriet had assigned the position and stayed with the number of men Joanna probably met in her work.

'She's on her own is what she said. She's also playing tennis,' Sam offered without enthusiasm, trying to defend his daughter against his own instincts.

'That figures,' Ted said.

'Yes. She placed third in a tournament.' Her father said this factually, third in a tournament, but he did not appear to have accepted it as a consolation prize for her leaving.

Ted suggested they all stay together for dinner that evening, his first such overture to them since the break-up, and they agreed. They went to a Chinese restaurant and Sam won the battle for the cheque, insisting on being the elder.

'I've got a good idea for a business,' Ted said over dessert, trying to enjoy the family unity. '*Mis*-fortune cookies. You open the cookie and it says something like "Don't ask." '

They did not think this was funny and lapsed into melancholy over the person missing from the table.

In saying good night, Harriet kissed Ted on the cheek awkwardly, not having done this for a while. Their plan was to come back the next morning and take Billy to the Statue of Liberty, an ambitious day for them, but they would not let Ted talk them out of it. This is why they had come – to be grandparents.

'Is he eating a lot of sweets?' Sam asked. 'He shouldn't have sugar.'

'I've got him on sugarless gum.'

'What about vitamins?'

'Every day, Sam.'

'They probably have sugar in them.'

'Well, I think you're doing a good job,' Harriet said.

'Yes, he is,' Sam added, still not up to referring to Ted in a personal sense.

'But – '

Ted waited for the disclaimer.

'– I think the child needs a mother.'

She said it with such pain over her daughter and despair in her voice, he could not possibly hear it as criticism of himself.

They arrived early the next day, ready to open the Statue of Liberty. Ted had not bothered to mention to them, as he had not mentioned it to anyone, that this day happened to be his fortieth birthday. He was not in the mood for a cake. They would be out with Billy until late afternoon. He had the time, but he could not decide on a suitable way to mark the day. Staying in bed was in first place.

This was a mild winter Sunday, however, and beginning to feel reflective about the event, he went out to stroll along the street, and on a whim – he went back. It was easy to do this, being a New Yorker, not having come here from another city. His childhood was a half-hour away by subway.

He took the train to Fordham Road and Jerome Avenue in the Bronx. He was standing near the elementary school he had first entered at age five, thirty-five years before. He walked home from school again.

The buildings, five-storey walk-ups, looked squat and

beaten, belonging to another architectural time. The little courtyards leading to the front entrances, a lost attempt at elegance, were now catchalls for litter. Graffiti were splattered across building walls. 'Tony D' said 'Up yours!'

Few people were on the street this Sunday morning. Three old women were on their way to church, and they scurried by two Spanish men in shirt-sleeves tinkering with a car motor. Ted walked past burnt-out stores, stepped around garbage and broken glass, the urban blight which had scarred much of the Bronx had reached into his old neighbourhood.

He arrived at his house, a walk-up on Creston Avenue near 184th Street. He sat down on his childhood stoop. He was astonished by how small everything looked. A two-sewer blast from home plate in stickball, which he remembered as a decent hit, was just a few yards long. The street where dozens of children played was a short, narrow block. The big hill nearby where they belly whopped and crashed into a snowdrift on the bottom was a little street with a slight downgrade. It was long ago and he must have been very little for it all to have seemed so large.

Across the street there had been a schoolyard where he played basketball. The basketball poles were gone, children did not play here now. A woman walked by, keeping a wary eye out for him, the stranger on the stoop, who might be there to mug her.

He sat, replaying stickball games in his mind, seeing ghosts on the corner, the guys, the girls. He hit a home run once in the schoolyard in pitching-in stickball off a fast ball from Stuie Mazlow, the best pitcher on the block, who watched in anger as the ball cleared the roof. He saw that home run all over again. These memories were vivid enough to still retain their shape thirty years later. And yet, in a few years, Billy, a baby, would have already reached the age the father had reached when he experienced these times. He pondered his perishability in second-generation home runs.

It was a decent time here, he decided, out of the house, anyway, in the street games. Billy was missing something, not having a stoop to sit on, and streets to play in which were not backed up with traffic, and an outfielder could actually hold a car in place with his hand, while the batter down the block took his swing, thirty years ago.

Billy was missing more than a neighbourhood. The child needs a mother, she said. How long could he hold on this way, without a woman in his life for Billy, for himself?

Hey, Mr Evans! An old man made his way along on the other side of the street. Remember me? I used to come to your candy store. I'm Teddy Kramer. Ralph's brother. I loved your egg creams. I'm in advertising. My wife left me. I'm divorced now. I've got a little boy. He's going to be five. I was five here once.

He had given himself a birthday present for suicides.

Ted walked over to the Grand Concourse and stopped in front of the Loew's Paradise, his old movie heaven, with stars and moving clouds on the ceiling. It was now split into three theatres, Paradise 1, Paradise 2 and Paradise 3.

'How can anything be Paradise Two?' he asked a maintenance man who was sweeping in front of the theatre.

'I don't know.'

'They should call it Paradise Lost.'

The man did not share Ted's need for historical perspective. He kept sweeping.

As Ted headed towards the subway, he saw a bloated man walking in his direction. The outlines of the face were familiar – Frankie O'Neill from the next block. The man squinted, recognizing Ted slowly.

'Frankie!'

'Is that you, Teddy?'

'It's me.'

'What are you doing around here?'

'Looking around.'

'I haven't seen you in –'

'A long time.'

'Holy cow! Where do you live?'

'Downtown. Yourself?'

'Hundred-eighty-third and the Concourse.'

'No kidding. Do you ever see any of the old people?'

'No.'

'What are you up to, Frankie?'

'Tending bar. In Gilligan's. It's still there. One of the few things around here that's still the same.'

'Gilligan's. Terrific,' he said, not wanting to offend the man with the fact that he had never even been in Gilligan's. 'Yourself?'

'I work in advertising.'

'What do you know? You married?'

'Divorced. I've got a boy. You?'

'Three kids. I married Dotty McCarthy. Remember her?'

'Oh, sure. Frankie – remember we had a fight once? And my jacket got caught up over my head and you were pounding the shit out of me?' Nine years old. A fight Ted would not forget. The aficionados of the block, brought up on Friday-night fights at the Garden, intervened, laughing at the ludicrousness of Ted flailing away, unable to see. He never forgot his embarrassment, a TKO, fight stopped for jacket over the head.

'A fight? You and me?'

'You don't remember?'

'No. Who won?'

'You did.'

'Well, sorry about that.'

'Paradise Two and Three. Isn't that a shame?'

'Yeah.'

And then they stood, awkwardly.

'Teddy, it's really good to see you. If you're around, stop by the bar. I'm on at five.'

'Thanks, Frankie. See you around.'

A drink in Gilligan's, where he had never been, in what remained of the old neighbourhood was not what he wanted on his fortieth birthday. He went back downtown on the subway, and watched a basketball game at home on television. Later, after Billy had gone to sleep, he toasted himself with a glass of cognac. Happy birthday, forty years old. At a time like this, what Ted really would have liked would have been to listen to *Gangbusters* on the radio while he sipped his chocolate milk.

CHAPTER TWELVE

Jim O'Connor phoned Ted and asked him to come into his office, and he entered to find O'Connor at nine-thirty in the morning with a bottle of scotch on the desk and two shot glasses.

'The drinks are on the house.'

'What's going on?'

'You're finished here, Ted.'

'*What?*'

'You're finished, I'm finished, we're all finished. The old man sold the company. You get two weeks' severance, and all of this week to use the office to find a job. Drink up.'

Ted poured himself a shot. He shuddered slightly, but it had little effect. He could have poured it into a blotter.

'He sold the company! Who's the buyer?'

'A group in Houston. They figure down there is where the real leisure areas are going to be. They bought the names of the magazines from the old man, and they're shifting everything down there. We're expendable. We don't know the territory.'

'But we know the business.'

'They want their own people. We're on the street.'

Employment agency people were faintly encouraging to Ted, but this was a specialized field, and he knew there were not many jobs. Three possible jobs were open at the time, he learned, all at far less money than he had been earning. He did not even know how he could take any of them. He would be operating at a loss. He went on interviews anyway, just to get the rhythm of being interviewed. For someone who wanted to get a new job before he had to let his family and friends know that he had lost the old one, the employment process was demoralizing. Hours and days passed with little movement as he was shuttled from one person to anther within a company. He registered for unemployment benefits. He carried a book to read wherever he went, so s not to stare at reception-room walls. By his third week of nemployment, as the interviews tailed off, on a Friday after-oon when he found himself with no appointments to keep, o phone calls to make, nothing practical he could do but wait or the Sunday classified section, and rather than read any onger or go to the movies, he elected to join Etta in the layground with Billy just to be doing something, he knew aat he was in deep difficulty.

He tried to ward off the feelings, to consciously make a ull-time job out of looking for work. He would get up early a the morning, dress as if for work, go downtown, use the 2nd Street Library as his office, make calls from the public hones there, stay busy, read between appointments. He ould circle ads, keep lists, visit employment agencies. But e was being worn down. There were days when he began the orning without anything meaningful to do until noon, when e was to call in to an employment agency. He would go arough the game of dressing and heading downtown with the orking people in order to get to the library, and once there, is only activity was to read the newspaper. And you were not ven allowed to read the newspaper in the 42nd Street Library they checked through your bags. He had to sneak the paper . He moved his office to a nearby branch where they let in ewspapers and had *Consumer Reports*. He could pass the me informing himself about products he would never need.

A worker at the unemployment office demanded to know hat he had done the day before specifically to look for ork, how many phone calls, how many interviews, where as the record, could this be verified? He had spent the ay at the library and made two phone calls.

'Why aren't you more flexible, Mr Kramer? Why don't ou try selling storm windows or something?' the man asked.

'It has limited potential. Winters are getting warmer. All ie seasons are flattening out.'

'Are you being sarcastic, Mr Kramer?'

'I'm looking for work. I need the money. Do you have ny idea how much Cheerios cost?'

'That's not the point – '

'Fifty-three cents and they're made out of air.'

He approved his claim, but with malice, giving Ted a clerical zinger. Ted was now being watched. Each week he would have to go through a long wait for an interview to prove to them that he was entitled to the money.

He determined it cost nearly $425 a week to live – for rent, utilities, dry cleaning, Etta, Cheerios. He had $95 a week coming from unemployment. Even when he was working, with the cost of a housekeeper, his expenses were high, and by the time his pay-cheque came, he needed that money. He never managed to save. He had a grand total of $1800 in the bank. In less than two months he would have exhausted all of his cash.

He told Etta that he was out of work and looking for a job, which she could see easily enough. She offered to let him defer the payment of her salary, but he preferred to continue to pay her for her time. He had not told Billy. The brown eyes did not miss a thing, however.

'Daddy, were you fired?'

'Where did you get that?'

'You're home sometimes now. And on *The Flintstones*, Fred was home, too. He got fired.'

'Do you know what fired means?'

'You don't have a job.'

'Well, I wasn't precisely fired. The company I worked for moved, and now I'm looking for a new job.'

'Oh.'

'And I'll have one soon.'

'Then can you play with me tomorrow?'

'It would be better if I look for work, Billy.'

He had now been out of work six weeks. He was down to the B level, sending his résumé to trade publications whose names he found in a reference book.

William Kramer was five years old. His birthday marked a full year of their lives since Joanna had left. Ted made the party. By request, a Batman cake and six special friends.

Ted noted that a miniature Batmobile for a gift and a modest party for a child cost $38.

He thought about taking temporary work, selling in a department store, telephone solicitation, but these would nullify his unemployment benefits. It did not pay to work at anything but his work. The money was disappearing. Everything was so costly.

'You lost your job. Ahhh!'

His intention had been to make a quiet announcement to his parents about his new position as soon as he got one. When his mother asked him directly, 'How is it going?' he knew the shortcut to a peaceful conversation was to say, 'Fine,' but he could not honestly say it.

'I'm afraid the company went under, Mother. We all lost our jobs. I'm looking. I'll get something.'

'He got fired. Fired!'

His father came to the phone.

'Ted, they fired you? Why did they fire you?'

'Listen, Dad, Fred Flintstone got fired. I was let go.'

'Who got fired?'

'The company was sold from under us.'

'They didn't take you with them? You must have done something bad for them not to take you with them.'

'They didn't want any of us. They relocated.'

'And now?'

'I'll find something.'

'He got fired. Ahhh!' His mother had taken over the play-by-play. 'Ted, you've got a baby to feed and that person to pay, and everything is big dollars today. And you're alone, no wife to help, God forbid anything should happen to you, what would the baby do? And you don't have a job! What are you doing to yourself?'

If she had left anything out, he could not think of it. He ended the conversation with assurances that his New York contingent would survive, and with his father shouting over from his end that maybe Ted should come to Florida and drive a cab – so many old folks didn't drive and couldn't

walk, there was good money in it – which appeared to Te
a rather total misreading of who he was.

An employment agency woman, who had greeted his résum
enthusiastically and said she would have him placed within
week, had not returned his calls for three weeks. Summe
was approaching. People were not leaving jobs, they wer
staying to get their vacation time. He was down to $900 i
the bank.

'Billy, goddammit, I told you to get out of here! I playe
with you! I played with you for a whole goddamn hou
after supper! I can't play with you any more. Go look at
book.'

'Don't shout at me.'

'Don't whine.'

'I'm not whining.'

'Beat it! Go to your room!'

He grabbed him and marched him out of the bedroom
his thumb and forefinger pressing into the child's arm s
deeply it left marks.

'You hurt me!' He started to cry.

'I didn't mean to hurt you. But I don't want you whinin
at me. Play by yourself, goddammit. Let me be.'

Work was at the core of his sense of self. He did no
consider himself gifted in any special way. It had taken hin
years to find this narrow area of commerce for himself. H
sold ideas in advertising, a space salesman. His job, his suit
and ties, his name printed on notepaper, the secretaries, th
modern offices, the money, which permitted him to keep going
try to forget her, hire the housekeeper, buy the wine – this
from work had sustained him. Without work, he felt im
potent.

And with the child, everything was so crucial, with thi
person so dependent upon him to be the daddy. He ha
been out of work before, but never with this feeling of anxiety
If Ted Kramer woke in the night, it was hours before h
could fall asleep again.

He had begun to reintroduce himself to employmen
agency people who had misplaced his résumé, filed his card

forgotten him in the cycle of new people, fresh out of work since he had been there – 'When did you say that was, Mr Kramer?'

Billy, wanting to help, offered solace, a sign from the cartoon character universe.

'Remember when Fred Flintstone got fired?'

'Yes, you told me about it.'

'Well, I was just watching, and Fred got a new job. Isn't that good, Daddy? That means you'll get a new job, too.'

He heard from Jim O'Connor. He had taken a trip to Europe with his wife and decided to return to the working world for one more job before retirement. He had joined a new magazine called *Men's Fashion*. O'Connor wanted to know if Ted was 'inside' or still 'out in the cold.' 'Out in the cold' seemed wildly inaccurate, since the weather turned an inclement 92 that day, and Ted had trudged through the humidity to an interview at a trade publication, *Packaging World*. O'Connor told him his longest stretch was during a recession in the fifties when he was 'out in the cold' for a solid year, a dubious bit of encouragement.

O'Connor could not promise anything – he was just getting established in the job – but he wanted Ted to work for him, if he could convince them to open up a slot, if he could get sufficient money, if Ted could wait a minimum of four weeks for him to try to set it up.

'It's kind of iffy. Let's talk again.'

'Just promise me you won't take anything crappy before I can do this.'

'I'll try not to take anything crappy.'

He was down to $600 cash. *Packaging World* was 'very interested' at nineteen, maybe they could go to twenty, a cut from what he had been earning. And they were making him jump through hoops. He had to prepare a mock sales call as if he were working for them – the make-believe client, an oily man in his sixties who was both the advertising manager and owner of the publication, a man who kept his eye on the till.

'Very nice. We'll let you know in a week or so.'

It was as if he had just sung 'Put on a Happy Face' at an audition.

'We haven't pinned down the pay.'

'Eighteen-five plus commissions.'

'You said nineteen, maybe twenty.'

'Did I? I must have made a mistake. No. Eighteen-five. And that's up from what we could get somebody for.'

'It's a little thin.'

'Well, we're not *Life* magazine.'

A cute remark, since *Life* magazine had folded, while *Packaging World* went on. So he had a possibility for a job, something two floors below crappy, he thought. Apart from Jim O'Connor's overture, this was all he could count on. If he took the job, he would probably have to move to an older building to reduce his rent. If he moved, the cost of moving would wipe out any savings from moving over the first year. In raw dollars, he nearly would do as well driving a cab. In New York, though, driving a cab was semi-hazardous duty. Cabbies often got held up on the job. He amused himself to think of this as one of the pluses for staying in his field. Few space salesmen got held up on the job. Then he began to think – what if something like that really happened to him? What if he got mugged somewhere or killed somehow? Where would that leave Billy? He realized he did not have a will. What if he died suddenly? Who would get the boy – his parents? Unthinkable. Joanna's parents? Impossible. Ted Kramer occupied himself with thoughts of his death. Then he decided to offer his child to the one person he felt he could trust in this way.

'Thelma, if I die – '

'Don't say that.'

'Listen to me. If some extraordinary thing happens and I die, will you take Billy?'

'That's the most touching – '

'Will you?'

'Do you mean it?'

'Yes, I do. I know it's not an easy thing to answer.'

'Ted – '

'Would you think about it?'

'I'm overwhelmed.'

'Well, if you think you could, I'd like to put it in my will.'

'Ted, don't talk like this.'

'I'd like to put it in my will.'

'You can, Ted. You can.'

'Thank you, Thelma. Thank you very, very much. He'd be all right with you. You're a good mother.'

Obsessed with the morbid, he called the lawyer and instructed him to draw up a will with Thelma named for Billy, and then he demanded that his doctor, whom he had not seen in two years, give him an emergency physical examination to confirm that he was not going to die by Tuesday. The doctor informed him that he seemed fit – the lab. reports would come through in a few days. On the next week-end morning, encouraged by his good health, he climbed in the playground with Billy in a spirited game of monkeys, an activity which still held a high position with Billy, Ted envisioning his son about to walk down the aisle, asking Ted to go to the playground for a quick monkeys before the ceremony, assuming Ted lived that long.

He could not afford to have Etta working for him beyond the next few weeks. Although she had offered to have him defer paying her salary, he was unable to accept having this lady subsidize his unemployment. And if he lingered in this situation, he would sink into the red with her. A year! O'Connor was once out a year. He might have to take care of Billy during the day himself and try to hire baby-sitters for the times he had interviews. He probably could qualify for a day-care centre at this point, or food stamps.

His brother, Ralph, called from Chicago. How was he doing, could he use some cash? He would have considered it a personal defeat to take anything from his older brother. He did not need any money, he told him. Ralph was coming in on business the following week and suggested they get together, go to a ball game. He put his wife, Sandy, on the phone, who pointed out they had not seen each other in over a year. She and Ralph were going to Florida with their children over the summer, perhaps Ted could bring Billy for a family reunion. He said he would consider it. But he did not know how he could possibly afford a trip to Florida.

The cupboard was nearly bare. The food bills were staggering. With survival instincts nurtured in his Bronx schoolyard – winners stay on, losers get off, you tried any moves to win – Ted Kramer put on what he thought of as The Gourmet Shuffle. He took a handful of credit cards from department stores, left over from Joanna's days and still in force since he did not owe the stores any money, and went on a wild buying spree. He went to any stores that had a food or a gourmet food department. Ted Kramer, who could not afford to buy chopped meat from a butcher or run up a large ord r at the supermarket, knew that he could buy food in a department store and the charges would not come through for weeks; he could pay them off on time. He began to buy prime meat on time, frozen vegetables, precious little peas twice the price of any he had ever bought, trout from Colorado, salmon from Washington, high-priced items, pasta from Italy, cookies from Scotland – 'Ma'am, this bread was actually flown in from Paris? Amazing. I'll take it.' Some he shipped home, some he carried, none he paid for with cash. Entire frozen dinners, veal marsala, paella; put up by a Mrs Worthington. Bless you, Mrs Worthington, for your distribution. Even essentials, eggs fresh from New Jersey, peanut butter. 'The frozen pizza? Is it really good or just frozen pizza? Fine. I'll take four.' He stuffed his freezer and overloaded the cabinets, piled up cartons in the front closet. If all else failed, they would have their chicken cacciatore, and he did not have to pay for any of it now, a little money at a time would do, so long as you paid them something. The stores just wanted to know you were still there. He was still there.

He met his brother, Ralph, at a Blarney Stone bar on Third Avenue. They were going to have an old-fashioned evening: beer and pastrami sandwiches at a bar, then out to Shea Stadium for the Mets against the Dodgers. Ralph was tall and muscular, handsome in a tough-guy way. He wore a silk suit, a thin striped tie and loafers. He could have passed for a television actor trying to pass for a mobster.

'You look skinny, Teddy.'

'I've been working on my weight.'

'Hey, bring this guy a Tab.'

'It's okay. I'll have a beer.'

'It sure has been a while.'

'I know.'

Ralph watched the legs of a passing girl through the window and then looked down at his food. Intimacy had never been a staple of this family and it did not appear to be on the table this night. Ted had the sinking sensation that one bite into the pastrami, they already had nothing to say to each other.

'Hey, Teddy, remember the old days – the Giants and the Dodgers for a three-game series? Friday night at the Polo Grounds or out at Ebbets Field?' Ralph offered, apparently feeling the same tension.

'Great times.'

Mercifully, they had old-time baseball to carry them along, Ernie Lombardi hitting 400-foot singles, ball games they went to when they were younger. This got them to the ball park, and then the ball game itself carried them along, as they talked about the hitters and the game in progress. During the seventh-inning stretch, Ralph said:

'Look at this place. All these shmuck-ass banners. What do they know about baseball?'

'And that organ music.'

'Come out to Chicago, Teddy. I can set you up in a liquor store.'

'Thanks, Ralph, but it's not what I do.'

'I don't mean *in* Chicago. In a suburb.'

'I appreciate it, Ralph, but no thanks.'

They returned to watching the game, and afterwards, jammed into a crowded subway train, they were spared the burden of further conversation on the way back to Times Square. They switched to old-time basketball on the walk back to the Hilton, where Ralph was staying.

'How about a drink?'

'It's too late. Billy gets up so early.'

'Is he okay?'

'He seems to be.'

'You got prospects?'

'A couple.'

'Teddy, you got to need some bread.'

He had his bread flown in from Paris.

'I'm fine, really.'

'How can you be?'

'I am.'

'Just say the word.'

'No, it's okay, Ralph.'

Money was time. He needed the time, he needed the money desperately and yet he could not bring himself to ask. In his mind, it would cost him too much to admit the need.

'It was a nice night, Ralph. Let's do it again when you come in.'

They shook hands, and suddenly Ralph squeezed his hand and would not let go.

'We're all so fucking distant in our family. Teddy –'

'You're here, Ralph. We had a good night.'

The veins began to swell in Ralph's forehead.

'Teddy! You got to need something!'

'I'm telling you, Ralph –'

Ralph reached inside his jacket pocket and pulled out his chequebook, his other hand squeezing Ted's arm.

'Don't say anything, Teddy. Don't move.'

'Ralph, I won't take it.'

'Teddy, let me do this thing.'

'No, Ralph.'

'I need to do this. Let me do this for you.' And he rushed to write a cheque before Ted could turn away from him, hurrying, folding it and shoving it into Ted's pocket.

'You can pay me back when you're rich.'

Ralph squeezed his brother in a half-hug, said, 'It's only money,' and walked on.

Ted did not look at the cheque. He could not bring himself to do it. He went home, sat at the dining-room table and finally unfolded the cheque on the table. He looked at it and then buried his head in his arms. The cheque was for $3000.

His brother had bought him time. In the morning, he could call *Packaging World* and tell them to take their lousy job and shove it.

Time magazine contacted him, and he spent several days seeing executives of the company, and everybody appeared to be impressed. There was one problem. A salesman in their West Coast office who originally said he did not wish to come to New York was now reconsidering. The man had priority.

It was maddening. He had a child to take care of. He felt he was not succeeding in what he considered a basic function, the business of being a provider.

He began walking downtown, thirty blocks to the library, and walking back uptown to keep from getting logy, and to save the car-fare. Charlie pressed a phone number on him. 'She's beautiful. Fantastic teeth. I'm doing her crown.' He said he had no money, no interest, no strength to start from the beginning with somebody and go through all the what-do-you-like?s and the what-don't-you-like?s.

Jim O'Connor called with a long explanation of how he spoke to the company president and they did not want a new salesman who would work on commission, since they wanted to reduce open-end costs – and Ted began to hold the phone away from his ear. I'll even take a quick no. Somebody, a quick anything. I can't stand all this waiting!

'And anyway, Ted, I had to agree. So it would be selling space, plus the details you're so good at – working with research, talking to the copy guys, like that.'

'Right.'

'It's just no commissions. I don't know what you'd call it. Sales and administration. Assistant to the advertising manager, I guess. Twenty-four thousand to start.'

'So when can you set it up?'

'It's set up.'

'So who do I see?'

'Nobody.'

'Come on, Jim!'

'It's my choice.'

'Jim –'

'You're my main man, Ted. Do you want it?'

'Yes, I want it!'

'Then you got it. You're hired. Ted, I'll see you Monday at nine-thirty.'

He hung up the phone and leaped through the air – 'Yahhah!' shouting and jumping like a football cheer-leader. Billy came running out of his room, where he was making a factory with his Tinker Toys.

'What is it, Daddy?'

'I got a job, little man! Your old man is out of the cold!'

'That's nice,' he said placidly. 'I told you, you would.'

'You sure did.' And he picked him up and spun him around and around in the air. 'Your daddy takes care! Yes, he does. We're going to be a-l-l r-i-g-h-t!'

But never again, my son. I don't want to ever live through anything like this again.

CHAPTER THIRTEEN

Men's Fashion magazine was on the stands, a stylish-looking publication with a large number of colour pages. The company was part of a conglomerate from South America with holdings in the apparel industry, and the directors of the company wanted a magazine that could help promote men's fashion. Ted was working with sales presentations he helped create, and he was off to a fast start with several contracts. He was pleased to remember he was good at what he did.

He returned the $3000 to his brother, along with a gift he found in a second-hand bookstore, *Who's Who in Baseball? 1944.* 'What ever happened to the St Louis Browns?' he wrote in his note. When he came to the salutation, he recalled the various detached ways he had chosen to sign off notes to his brother in the past – 'Best,' 'Regards,' 'See you.' This time he was able to write 'Love, Ted.'

He registered Billy in a day camp for the summer, on

Thelma's recommendation. Kim had attended the previous summer, the last summer of Thelma and Charlie's marriage.

'Charlie's not too happy about the money this year,' she said. 'I think what he'd like for us to do is sit in the apartment all summer with the air-conditioner off.'

Ted attended a parents' meeting for the '5's' one afternoon during his lunch hour. It turned out to be a mommies' meeting – he was the only man in the room. He sat with the women and met Billy's counsellors, a boy and a girl who were in college and who looked to Ted as if they were fourteen. Ted took notes – Billy had to have name tapes, extra sneakers and a change of clothes. He sensed the others staring at him. What do you think, folks, a widower? Unemployed while my wife works? I bet you'd never guess. As the head counsellor described a typical day at camp, Ted became nervous. A swimming-pool, was that safe? An entire day, would Billy be lonely? His Billy was going to be leaving the city in a bus, taken by strangers to a place outside somewhere, more than a cab ride away. And in the fall, Billy would start school, real school, with Board of Education door knobs and Assembly days and the Pledge of Allegiance. *They* would be taking over. His precious primitive was going to be institutionalized, his edges rounded out, another little face on the milk line. Billy was going off to camp and then to school, and Ted was having separation anxieties.

Ted would wait with Etta in the mornings for the camp bus, but Billy was already embarrassed about kissing his father goodbye in front of the other children. Shaking hands seemed too grown up – Ted wasn't ready for that. He settled for patting Billy on the back.

The outside world was making its presence felt, children were raising questions, and so was Billy.

'Daddy, where is Mommy?'

'Your mommy is in California.'

'Is she re-married?'

'Re-married? She's not re-married, as far as I know. Who used that word?'

'Carla in my camp. Her parents are divorced and her

mommy is re-married.'

'Yes, that happens. Somebody gets married again to somebody new.'

'Are you going to re-married?'

'I don't know.'

'Are you going to re-married Phyllis?'

Phyllis? The lawyer. He had nearly forgotten her.

'No, Billy.'

'Daddy?'

'Yes, Billy?'

'Will you and Mommy re-married?'

'No, Billy. Daddy and Mommy will never re-marry.'

Jim O'Connor told Ted to take two weeks' vacation time and he expected him to get away.

'Maybe.'

'Ted, you've been working your ass off. Don't you have anybody in your life to tell you you're run down?'

He ruled out Fire Island, not wishing to be in the audience for any more nervous breakdowns. He looked through the travel ads, special packages based on double occupancy. That was Ted, double occupancy, he and his shadow. On a trip, Billy would never be out of his sight, unless Ted attempted to hire a chambermaid to baby-sit so he could look for pick-ups at the bar. Not exactly a class vacation. He was tired. The jobless period had exhausted him, he had been working hard, and he knew that an intensified time alone with Billy making typical children's demands was not rest and rehabilitation. He eventually decided to take two weeks in August, spend the first week with Ralph and the family in Florida, a reunion was long overdue, and then he would return to New York for a week. With Billy in day camp full days, he could be alone to rest, nap, go to movies, stay home, eat chocolate-chip ice-cream in bed and watch daytime movies on television, and just relax.

On the way to the airport, he revealed the big news, which he had confirmed with his sister-in-law.

'Billy, when we get to Florida, we're also going to Disneyworld.'

The boy's eyes enlarged. He had seen the Disneyworld commercials on television.

'Yes, William Kramer. You are going to meet Mickey Mouse.'

They were met at the airport by Ralph and Sandy, and Dora and Harold, who greeted Billy with kisses authentic and chocolate, a bag of candy which would have made the child's other grandparents apoplectic. His mouth full of sweets, he loved Fort Lauderdale. The plan was to sleep in a nearby motel and for everyone to spend the days at the pool in Dora and Harold's complex. After checking in, they linked up with Ted's niece and nephew. Sandy had been a showgirl in Chicago, a tall long-legged redhead who kept most of the old men poolside in a coronary danger zone whenever she came down for a visit. Their eldest, Holly, was also tall with attractive features, and at sixteen had already refined adolescence into a smoky sulk. The young lifeguard was in love — drownings could have occurred at his feet. Their other child, Gerald, fifteen, was a strong, gangling boy, who was cannonballing into the pool. They acknowledged Ted with teenage 'Oh, hi's.

'Billy is a fabulous-looking kid,' Sandy said. 'But you look terrible.'

'Give me a chance. I haven't had my mother's cooking yet. I'll look worse.'

'Cooking? I'm not doing any cooking,' Dora said over her shoulder without missing a beat, while talking to friends at the pool. 'I wouldn't cook for all you people.'

'We're all going out for dinner on Ralph,' Harold announced.

'Ralph, I don't want you bankrolling my stay here,' Ted said.

'Forget it. I'm writing a lot of it off.'

'How are you going to do that?'

'Easy.'

Ralph approached one of Dora and Harold's friends, a bony octogenarian sunning himself on a chaise lounge.

'Mr Schlosser, I meant to ask you. Would you be interested in a liquor delivery route in Chicago?'

'You kidding? I wouldn't be interested in a walk to the grocery.'

'Thank you. There, Ted – it goes in a diary. "Discussed liquor route with S. Schlosser in Florida." I just made this a business trip.'

'There is a certain sense of humour in our family.' He indicated his parents. 'Not always intentional, but it's there.'

'That's my Ralph, a big liquor executive,' Dora was saying a while later. 'And that's my Ted, he sells men's clothes.'

Billy played in the overflow of the pool with a toy boat, but when several children jumped into the pool, splashing water, he scurried back to Ted's chair.

'We're inseparable,' he said to Sandy, with a mixture of pride and annoyance.

Ted had asked for a conference with Billy's teacher before the nursery school term ended, and she said she felt he had adjusted well. 'He seems to be a perfectly normal child.' He focused on the 'seems to be.' 'Does he have any problems that you can see?' 'No,' she said. 'What about being too timid?' 'Every child is different. Some parents feel their children are too aggressive.' And now Billy was on his lap, hardly too aggressive. He realized he might, in fact, be watching him too closely, but this was unavoidable with the boy sitting on him.

He slept about three hours that night, Billy snored, the air-conditioner rattled. At eleven the next morning, Billy discovered he, too, could cannonball into the pool, provided Ted caught him before he went under. After a half-hour of this, Ted was so exhausted his hands were trembling. Several skirmishes took place over toys between Billy and other children. He lost his toy boat to another child and Ted intervened with sandbox diplomacy, unable to watch while his child cried so bitterly over the loss.

'If it's yours, stand up for it!' he shouted at him.

'You have no right to yell at me,' Billy protested in tears.

After negotiating magazine deals in New York he had come to Florida to negotiate toy boats and was not doing it very successfully. Sandy, who had been observing, asked

Holly to take Billy to the nearby swings.

'I got you ten minutes.'

'Thanks, Sandy.'

'I don't like what I see. I was talking to Ralph – and I think you need a little time away. The kid, too. Sometimes parents and kids need a little time away from each other.'

'You're very uptight,' Ralph said.

'Here's what we'll do and don't say no. We'll all go to Disneyworld and we'll take Billy. You can do what you like. Stay here, go to Miami, check into a hotel. He'll be fine with us. It'll be good.'

'I'm not sure. Let me think about it.'

Involuntary erections settled the decision. In his nylon bathing-suit, with Billy moving around in his lap, Ted was getting involuntary erections. They were uncomfortable and embarrassing, and when Billy sought out Ted's lap again and Ted got another one, he had an overwhelming desire for freedom from involuntary erections. Let Billy sit on Mickey Mouse's lap for a while.

When Ted informed Billy he would be going on to Disneyworld with the rest of the family, while Ted would be taking a few days by himself, the child looked betrayed.

'It was supposed to be our time together.'

'We have a lot of time together.'

'I don't want to go.'

'To Disneyworld? Actual Disneyworld?'

A stacked deck. He could not resist actual Disneyworld. The family settled into a rented station-wagon for the drive north, Dora attempting to sweeten the pot with a large bag of brown and red licorice for Billy. 'Don't worry. He'll be okay,' Dora shouted. 'Eat your candy.' Billy waved a forlorn goodbye from the window, the first time father and son had ever been separated.

They would be at Disneyworld for three days. Ted could meet them when they returned or he could stay away for the rest of the week, since Sandy was staying on. He could also be away for the following week, but that would mean Billy would be in the exclusive care of Ted's parents, and he had a reluctance about leaving him that long in candyland.

Harold was not exactly Dr Lee Salk. In one of the poolside toy arguments, when Ted was groping for a solution, Harold called over, 'Tell him to punch in the belly. That gets 'em. You gotta teach that kid to punch in the belly.' But he was free. He could barely remember how long it had been since he had this much freedom. He could have a *voluntary* erection, sleep until 10 a.m. He could have a liaison with the Widow Gratz, a youngish woman, perhaps not even fifty, he judged – the best-looking local lady at the pool, a still-trim figure, appealing, if one overlooked the plastic hair piled up on her head. He had caught himself eyeing the Widow Gratz, but of course if word of such a peccadillo ever reached his parents, they would be lighting candles for him – 'You did what?' Still, he was free to even have such thoughts.

He chose not to spend any more time in the Fort Lauderdale-Miami area. In New York he had seen a series of ads for a new resort hotel on the west coast of Florida. The Shells, patterned after the Club Mediterranee, one price for all facilities. The place looked attractive and it was in Sarasota, a short flight away. The Widow Gratz he would just have to leave to Mr Schlosser. He phoned the hotel and made a reservation through Sunday morning. The next flight was early evening, and he left Fort Lauderdale travelling much lighter than when he came.

The Shells was a modern facility at the beach, a strip of attached rooms, motel style, overlooking the water, with a screened-in dining terrace and bar, and a swimming-pool. He was led to the dining area, where dinner was being served buffet-style and it was immediately apparent that The Shells was fresh-paint new and two-thirds empty. The people scattered about the room seemed to be from a convention of airline pilots, so uniformly clean-cut they all were. He took a seat at a table of eight, five healthy-looking men and three healthy-looking women, and managed to feel simultaneously swarthy and green.

He learned that The Shells had become a spa for local Delta and Eastern employees and the people at his table who looked like pilots were pilots. Arriving on a Tuesday, he was out of the flight pattern – there seemed to be several ongoing relationships at the table. The discotheque opened at 10:30 p.m. He did not know if he could stay awake that long. He had a drink at the bar and noted another demographic pocket among the guests, New Yorkers, about a dozen people, shorter, stouter, tenser than the air wing, who were clustered together for warmth. He did not want to go through any New York talk. When only a few people showed up at the discotheque, mostly couples, he went back to his room, expecting to sleep until noon. His internal mechanism, tuned to five years of Billy, woke him at 7:15.

Ted ate breakfast in an empty dining-room and then walked down to the beach, spectacular in the morning light. Disneyworld was baby-sitting for Billy. No one was pulling at Ted's hand. No one was making demands. He had no responsibility other than to himself. He raced into the water and swam for a while, peacefully alone. When he came out, he stood on the shore and feeling his surge of freedom, released a Johnny Weissmuller a-a-h-a-a-h-a-h! terrifying a flock of small birds in the trees behind, who had never seen a jungle movie and who took off in the direction of Miami.

During his stay, he never mentioned Billy. A few times, when the talk was personal, he said he was divorced. He did not wish anyone to know more than that – no complicated discussions, no explanations, no Billy. This worked externally. But Billy was still on his mind. He wanted to call on several occasions, see if he was all right, talk to him. He resisted, though. He had left a number. They could reach him in an emergency.

Several of the pilots organized volleyball games on the beach and Ted, of Fire Island, had instant respectability. He was 'Ted, boy,' to Bill and Rod and Don; 'Ted, honey,' to Mary Jo and Betty Anne and Dorrie Lee in the coed games. The days became a blur. He swam, played volleyball, swam, played volleyball, ate, swam. The nights evolved to Dorrie Lee, a cute young woman of twenty-four from Jacksonville, who had never been north of Washington, and worked Atlanta-Miami as a stewardess. They would make love in his room and then she would go back to her room to sleep because she was sharing with Betty Anne and did not want to get a reputation. He was to have difficulty later recalling anything specific they discussed. It was all the most immediate, casual talk, how nice the day, how much fun the volleyball, how good the dinner. They discussed their professions very little. He did not tell her about Billy. On Saturday morning, when she checked out to return to work, she thanked him for helping to make it a wonderful vacation, and he thanked her for the same. They exchanged numbers and would call if they were in either of their respective cities, concluding a near-perfect limited commitment vacation relationship, semi-tropical and semi-romantic.

On Sunday, he returned to Fort Lauderdale. He got out of a cab outside the complex and walked towards the pool. Sandy saw him first and waved. Billy emerged from behind a beach chair and came running. He ran full speed in his choppy, unformed gait, yelling, 'Daddy! Daddy!' on the long walkway from the pool, and then he jumped into his father's arms. As the boy chattered away about shaking hands with Mickey Mouse, and Ted carried him back towards the others, he knew that for all his need to get away, to be alone, to get him out of his arms – above all else, he had missed him very much.

CHAPTER FOURTEEN

He was in a class of thirty-two children, no longer the only Billy in his immediate universe, which Billy R. would have to learn, as well as the two Samanthas. Ted walked with the boy to school on the first day, the entrance to the building crowded with children hugging, jumping, hitting. Parents were outsiders with their 'Now, now, that's enough's which were largely ignored. Billy was cautious, and Ted led him up the steps of the building to Kindergarten in Room 101 – he seemed to remember a Room 101 in his life somewhere. Ted stayed a few minutes and then left – 'Mrs Willewska will pick you up. See you later, big boy.' Billy was in the system. Regardless of Ted's feelings about separation and the passing of time, he had a sense of accomplishment – he got Billy here. He looked just like the other children. You couldn't tell a difference.

Thelma gave Ted low grades on his fall social life.

'You're withdrawing. You're not going out again.'

'I have six phone numbers, a girl I can see if I'm ever in Atlanta-Miami, and I have my eye on one of the mothers from Billy's class, who looks like Audrey Hepburn in *Roman Holiday* and doesn't wear a wedding ring.'

'So long as you stay in circulation. It's good for –'

'What, Thelma?'

'I don't know. My mother always used to say it. I guess it's good for the circulation.'

He approached Samantha G.'s mother one morning and asked if she would have time for a cup of coffee. They went to a nearby coffee shop where they began by talking about children and then she informed him she was divorced, but she was seeing someone, maybe their housekeepers could get the children together. So his Audrey Hepburn had made a coffee date to get a cookie date for her daughter. He understood. The children needed their social lives, too.

He joined the parents' association at school to be a concerned parent and signed up for the communications committee, which meant he asked his company's art department to run off a handbill for Open School Week. At a class meeting, Ted Kramer sat on a tiny chair under an oak-tag rendering of 'Our friends, the seasons.' Billy's teacher was a Mrs Pierce, a young woman in a dress from India. She touched off fantasies in Ted relating to his own Mrs Garrett on up to Mrs Bienstock, and he wanted to take Mrs Pierce and feel her up in the clothing closet to the smell of steam from the radiator and wet galoshes.

Rumours began to circulate through Ted's company. The directors were said to be dissatisfied with profits in the American magazine industry. The chairman was said to have told someone they might discontinue publication within the month.

Ted was furious. He could be out of a job again. It was deeply upsetting to him how little influence he had over such a central concern as his own livelihood. He had been working hard and successfully and now he could be on the street in that desperate situation all over again.

Jim O'Connor placed a call to the board chairman in Caracas. The following morning a cable arrived for use internally and outside the company stating that there were no plans whatsoever to discontinue publication. However, advertisers became aware of the rumours and were cautious. Several cancelled their schedules. Assured by management of a resolve to continue, Ted and O'Connor attempted to restore advertisers' confidence. By sheer will, Ted was going to save the company and his job. While O'Connor was calling on his contacts, Ted began making as many sales calls as possible, he wrote copy for a new sales presentation, he pushed a market research study to be completed, he wrote a sales presentation from the survey, he even conceived a men's fashion show outdoors on Madison Avenue to demonstrate that they were still in business. For three weeks, he worked days and nights and gradually, some of the negative talk was overcome and new orders began to come in. Ted had helped to avert a crisis. The company was still functioning and he would have a job for a while. What he did not have was a clear way out of money-survival problems. He could still conceivably be out of work again and he had built his bank balance up to only $1200. In an article in *The New York Times* it was estimated that it now cost $85,000 to bring up one child in New York City through the age of eighteen. And they did not even count in the cost of a housekeeper.

His friend, Larry, meanwhile, was prospering. He and Ellen bought a house on Fire Island.

'How do you get to that, Larry?'

'Well, a hot streak at the office. And we got two incomes, don't forget.'

Two incomes, the magic number. He had begun to see someone with her own income, a designer at an art studio. Vivian Fraser was an attractive woman of thirty-one, poised, sophisticated, maybe $20,000 a year, he figured. She probably would have been dismayed to know that for all the care she took with her appearance, at least one man thought that what she looked like was – solvent.

He also entered her without her knowledge in the What Kind of Mommy Might She Be Sweepstakes. It was intriguing to him to think an outside force could bring both emotional stability and fiscal responsibility into the house. But anyone he brought into the house would eventually arrive in his bedroom, and anything from juice to a bad dream could bring the house detective into the room with his people, and Ted could never be certain his people could get along with Billy's people and he did not even know how to avoid these considerations.

After Billy and Vivian had met briefly one evening, Ted asked Billy, 'Did you like Vivian?' realizing this was meaningless, since what he really wanted to hear was 'Oh, yes, a fine woman. I feel I can relate to her on a one-to-one basis, and as you know, a commercial artist can always augment our income, in addition to her emotional presence.'

'Uh-huh,' the boy said.

Larry and Ellen invited Ted and Billy to come out to Fire Island to see the new house and spend a week-end. Another couple was also invited with their ten-year-old daughter. The children played on the beach, the grown-ups drank champagne. Ted was relaxed, except for wishfulness. He would have loved such a luxury, a beach house – and the car for the getaway week-ends, and the warm-weather vacations in the winter, and the other luxuries they would never have . . . $85,000 to age eighteen – with no one other than himself paying child support. If a Good Fairy out of one of Billy's nursery tales appeared on the deck of the beach house in a hooded sweat shirt and said, 'What may I grant thee?' he would have said, 'To get six months ahead.'

The weather turned raw in the city. Week-end outdoor activity was going to be limited, and city parents would be relying on their inner resources and museums. Ted took it upon

himself to entertain three of Billy's friends at home on a
Saturday – Kim and two of Billy's classmates – for lunch
and an afternoon of play. The child would have buddies and
in turn, their parents would reciprocate. He was the referee
for occasional disputes, but for the most part stayed in the
bedroom reading, guarding against his temptation to check to
see if Billy was standing up to the others. They all seemed
to be content. Left on their own, they organized themselves
into dress-up games, hide-and-seek, and they took turns in
the adventures of The Children Eaters. He heard the sound
of chewing – friendly chewing, he presumed. For several
hours, he had a play group in his apartment. When the
mothers appeared to claim their $85,000-through-age-eighteen
parcels he delivered them intact, pleased with his administration of the day.

'Presenting the fantastic Super Jet' – Billy announced from
his room – 'with the secret of its fantastic speed!'

Earlier, Ted had heard the children discussing the construc-
tion of an aeroplane of Billy's, and they had apparently taken
the metal toy apart as a scientific experiment.

'Here it comes!' Billy burst out of the room flying his
plane, making a whirring sound, holding the disassembled
toy in his hand. When he reached the door, he tripped on
the doorstep and fell forward. Ted was standing in the hall
a few feet away and saw him coming straight at him, as if
in a sequence he could not stop – the body hurtling forward,
the fall, the impact, the elbow hitting the floor and then
driven upward, the metal piece in his hand, the scream –
'Daddy!' the metal like a razor. It ripped into the boy's
skin at the cheekbone, slashing upwards from the outside of
his cheek to his hairline, blood leaking into the boy's eyes
and across his face. For an instant, Ted was frozen. He saw
it, but he could not have seen it. 'Daddy, I'm bleeding!' he
cried, and Ted was already over him, cradling him, carrying
him, grabbing towels, 'It's all right, baby. It's all right,
baby,' fighting off the feeling he was going to faint, rocking him – ice, he needed ice, it helps a wound – patting his
head, kissing him, dabbing the blood with ice and the towels,
his shirt covered with blood, Don't faint – I think I'm going

to faint – checking him over, trying to see the damage through the blood. 'It's stopping, Billy. You're going to be all right.' And he rushed out into the street and hailed a cab to the hospital, patting the sobbing child, cradled in his arms.

At the emergency ward they were behind a broken arm of a teenager and an old woman who had fallen, but Billy was actually next, the attendant informed Ted, 'because he needs the surgeon.' Surgeon? It stopped bleeding so quickly, he thought it might not be so bad, after all. He had taken Billy to the hospital where his pediatrician maintained an office, and he asked the attendant to call up to see if the doctor was in the building. Billy had stopped crying and he watched every movement of the people around him on guard for whatever terrible thing might happen next.

Ten stitches were required to close the wound, a line from the topmost part of his cheek, running nearly parallel to his sideburn. The surgeon applied a head bandage and said to Billy, 'Don't go knocking your head against any walls, little fella. And don't take any showers, okay?' 'Okay,' he said in a frightened, quiet voice. By chance, the pediatrician had been in his office and he came down. He gave Billy a lolly for being brave and then Ted had Billy wait outside the room for a few moments.

'You're lucky. Our best man was on,' the pediatrician said.

'Will it leave a bad scar, do you think?' Ted asked in a whisper.

'Any time the skin is broken, you can have scarring,' the surgeon said.

'I see.'

'I did my best – but, yes, there will be a scar.'

'Think of it this way, Mr Kramer,' the pediatrician said. 'He's a very fortunate boy. One inch and he could have lost an eye.'

Billy picked at his hamburger that night. Ted had a double scotch on the rocks for dinner. They went through the normal rituals of the night, time to brush teeth, time for a story, both trying to create a normalcy to neutralize the event. Ted put him to sleep early and the child did not protest, exhausted by the tension.

I was so near. If only I could have caught him.

Ted went through the house wiping up blood stains. He took Billy's clothes, which he had tossed to the side along with his shirt and the towels and stuffed them down the incinerator. He could not stand looking at them. At 11 p.m. while trying to watch the news, seeing it happen all over again, Ted got up and vomited scotch and bile into the toilet bowl.

He could not come close to sleeping. In the next room, Billy was having tortured dreams, whimpering in his sleep. Ted came and sat on the floor beside the bed.

Scarred for life. Scarred for life. He was repeating it to himself as though the words 'for life' had some additional meaning. He began to replay the fall, if only he had come into the room earlier, seen the toy, anticipated what Billy was going to do, been nearer, caught him, not planned a day like this, he got too tired, he might not have tripped . . .

He sat there, holding a vigil, thinking back. How did he get here – with this child who was so connected to him? In the beginning, when Joanna was first pregnant, the baby did not seem to have a connection to him, and now, the child was linked to his nervous system. Ted could feel the pain of the injury so acutely that his body could very nearly not absorb the pain. Was there a turning point, a moment when his life might have been different? If he had stayed with one of the others? Who were the others? Who would he have been? Who would his child have been? Would there have been more than one child? No children? What if he had not gone to that one beach house party that night? If he had not said exactly what he said to the man with Joanna? If he had not called her, who would he be with now? Would his life have been different? Better? Was there a smoking gun? Would he have been happier if none of it had happened the way it did? Then Billy would not exist. Would he have been better off if Billy did not exist? The boy whimpered in his sleep and he wanted to gather him up in his arms and make him sleep more peacefully, which was not within his power.

There was no one moment when it might have been different or better, he decided. It is not that simple. And there are accidents. Billy, Billy, I would have caught you if I could.

After keeping him out of school for a few days, Ted released Billy, who wore his white bandage like a symbol of bravery. 'You had ten stitches?' Kim said in awe. 'A tight healing,' the surgeon pronounced. The boy was left with an indentation of the skin, four inches long on the right side of his face, not marring the child's appearance, but a scar nonetheless. Ted's healing went more slowly. He would think about the fall. It would flicker across his consciousness at odd times and he would shudder, a knife-like pain in his bowels. As a catharsis he told some of the people he knew about the accident, reinforcing the positive: 'It was tremendously lucky. He could have lost an eye.' He would get to telling the grandparents later.

Ted was at the zoo with Charlie, the children going around on a pony cart ride.

'It's like with teeth,' Charlie said. 'A person chips a tooth and thinks the whole world is looking at that chipped tooth. Or he has a silver crown in the back of his mouth and he thinks everybody can see it.'

'Wouldn't you have noticed the scar? Really, Charlie?'

'Maybe not. Maybe only if you told me.'

'I see it. Sometimes I see it when my eyes are closed.'

'Daddy, a kid in school told me his brother told him that a hockey player got twenty stitches.'

'Hockey can be a rough game. They get hurt sometimes.'

'Could I have a hockey stick?'

'I don't know. They're for older kids.'

'I won't play on ice. Just by the house.'

'Boom-boom Kramer over here.'

'What do you mean, Daddy?'

'Boom-Boom Geoffrion – he was a hockey player. When you're a little older I guess you can have a hockey stick if you still want one.'

'How old do you have to be when you don't sleep with your

Teddy and your people any more?'

'No special age. Whenever you want.'

'I think I'm old enough. I think I'd like to try not to sleep with them.'

'If that's what you want –'

'Well, they can still stay in my room. Sort of like statues. And I can still play with them during the day. But they can be on my bookcase and watch me when I'm sleeping.'

'When do you want to do that?'

'Tonight.'

'Tonight?'

The night his son gave up his Teddy, the father was feeling the sentiment more than the child. Billy was very proud of himself the next morning, having slept through the night without a baby's security. He was passing through crises. He went about his days at full speed without caution. When he raced through the house or in the playground, Ted was apprehensive. 'Careful, Billy, not so fast.' 'Not so fast' held no meaning. Billy had forgotten the fall, the stitches. He was five and growing.

But the injury lingered for Ted. He would never forget the moment. The piece of metal like a razor cutting open the boy's face. The blood. And the end of self-delusion – that his child was perfect, that his beautiful face was to bear no scars, that the child was to bear no scars. His son whom he loved so deeply was imperfect, perishable. He could be hurt again. He could die. Ted Kramer had envisioned a safe, controlled world for his son. The wound was testimony. He could not exercise such control.

CHAPTER FIFTEEN

Ted Kramer returned to the office after meeting with a client and was given his telephone messages. Joanna Kramer had called. She asked that he call back and left a local number. His work day was effectively terminated at that moment.

'This is Ted.'

'Oh, hello, Ted. How are you?' she said warmly. 'This is a new job, isn't it?'

'Yes, it's a new job. How did you get the number?'

'From your housekeeper.'

'You called the house?'

'I didn't upset Billy, if you're worried. I called when he was at school.'

'Yes, he is at school.'

'Yes, I know.'

'Joanna, could we get to it? I'm pretty busy.'

'Well, I'm in New York and there are some things I'd like to talk to you about. I don't think they should be said over the phone. Could we meet for a drink?'

'What things?'

'When can I see you?'

He could spar with her on the phone, put her off, hang up, but just as his day was over the moment she called, he did not think he could delay knowing why she called.

'Today is probably best for me.'

'Good. There's a new place – Slattery's, on 44th Street –'

'Right.'

'See you there at six, okay?'

'Right.'

'It's nice to talk to you again, Ted.'

'It is? Why?'

He shuffled papers at his desk, called Etta and asked her to stay on, looked at some trade papers and then left work at five. He stopped in a bar on the way and had a drink in preparation for his drink.

Slattery's was a narrow bar with several tables in the back. He moved past the bar to the rear, and Joanna was waiting at a table. She did not have a tan, as in her last time through. She was wearing a sweater and skirt, and she could have been any of the working women who were in the room, except of course, she was the prettiest woman in the room.

'Hello, Ted. You look well.'

'You do, too.'

They ordered vodka martinis from the waiter, and Ted sat back, permitting her to take the lead. She seemed nervous.

'How is this new job, Ted?'

'Fine.'

'That's good.'

She was after something, he was sure.

A couple took seats at a nearby table.

'Look at us, Joanna. Just like any old couple out for a drink. Who would believe it?'

'Well, I guess you want to know why I called you here.' She smiled, but he did not respond, his throat muscles pulling with tension. 'Ted, I've been living in New York for the past two months.'

'You have?'

'I've got an apartment on East 33rd Street —'

'That's extraordinary. You've been living here?'

She was awkward, fumbled with her drink. Was this an overture? Was she here to broach a reconciliation? he wondered. Last time that was certainly not her intent, but this was nearly a year later.

'Things change. I'm working for the Grand Central Racquet Club. Sort of a girl Friday. And I get in some free court time.'

'It seems to me you've put a lot of people through a lot of shit so you can get yourself some free court time.'

'I suppose you think of it that way. How is Billy?'

'He's great . . . except . . . he fell . . .' He needed to tell her, nearly as a confessional. 'And he cut his face. He has a scar, Joanna, from here to about here.'

'Oh.'

'It's lucky it wasn't worse.'

They were both silent, the closest they had been since the break-up to shared feelings.

'You can't tell from a distance, Ted.'

'What?'

'I've seen him.'

'You have?'

'A few times I sat in a parked car across from the school and watched you take him to school.'

'Really?'

'He looks like he's a great kid.'

'You sat in a car?'

'Watching my son ...'

Her voice trailed off. The loneliness of the scene, Joanna in a car across the street, got through to Ted and he shook his head.

'I couldn't do anything more. I was thinking it out, trying to make my decision –'

So she does want to reconcile! That's why she's trying to be so friendly.

'Ted – I want Billy back. We can work out an arrangement so you can see him on the week-ends, but I want custody.'

'You want him *back*?'

'I've established residence here in New York. I'll live here in New York with him. It wouldn't be right to separate you two.'

'Are you kidding me?'

'I want my son. I'm not sitting in cars looking at him from across the street any more.'

'You've got to be kidding.'

'I am not.'

'The time I've put in! What I've lived through! And now you want him *back*?' He was raising his voice.

'We can discuss this pleasantly!'

People had begun to look at them as the almost-like-any-other couple in the bar moved into their own special category.

'And I'm finally getting organized, finally – and now you want to take him away from me?'

'I'm not shutting you out. You'll still see him. On week-ends. You'll see him, Ted. You're his father –'

'And what are you?'

'I'm his mother. I'm still his mother. I never gave that up. You can't.'

'Joanna, go fuck yourself!'

'Ted, I'm trying to be direct with you. There are other ways I could have gone about this.'

'I mean it. That may not be the most articulate thing in

the world to say, but there it is. Go fuck yourself!'

'Ted, there are courts of law. I have legal recourse –'

'I don't want to discuss it. What I want to discuss is who is paying for this drink?'

'What are you talking about?'

'Who pays the bill for this? Do I? Do I get stuck again? Do you invite me to have a drink with you – to listen to what *you* want – and am I supposed to pay?'

'Who pays for the drink is meaningless. I'll pay.'

'Yes. That's right. You'll pay. Waiter!'

The waiter was standing nearby, having come close to listen to the juicy scene at table three.

'I want another. On the double!'

'Yes, sir.'

'You're paying. I'm drinking.'

'Ted, you're just being angry –'

'What else do I get? Can I have a sandwich from the counter? Are you buying that, too, or just the drinks?'

'You can have anything you want.'

'You're a big spender.'

'Ted, I'm going through with this. I've had time to think. I've been through some changes. I've learned some things about myself.'

'What did you learn? I'm really interested to know.'

'Nothing that specific.'

'One thing. Tell me one thing, that *I've* paid for – that *you've* learned.'

'That I never should have married you.'

She said it softly, without any particular cruelty in her voice, as a statement of fact as much for herself as for him. He was so devastated by the finality of her feelings, his anger was momentarily defused. The waiter appeared with the drink and put it in front of Ted, who just sat looking at it.

'Put it on the lady's bill,' he said. 'She's paying,' and he got up and walked out of the bar, leaving her there.

He snapped at Billy for a variety of minor transgressions that evening and sent him off to bed, not having the patience to read him a story or fill his time-killing requests for more apple juice.

'You're in a bad mood.'

'I had a bad day. I would like this day to end as quickly as possible. You'll help by going to bed *now*.'

She wants him back! He wished he had the moment in the bar again, to take that drink and throw it in her face.

The phone rang and it was Vivian, calling about tickets for the ballet, which she was going to try to get, and for an instant he did not know who she was or what she was saying. She didn't get the tickets, should they go to a movie? A movie, the ballet, what was the difference? He did not care what he was going to be doing Friday night at eight o'clock.

'Fine, a movie is fine. Wonderful.'

'Are you all right?'

'I'm not feeling terrific.'

'What's wrong?'

'Nothing. I'll talk to you later in the week.'

'What is it, Ted?'

'Nothing.'

'Really – '

'My ex-wife just showed up in New York and wants custody of my son.'

'Oh – '

Vivian probably would have been satisfied with – 'I've got the flu,' or 'I've got someone with me' – even that – but this was very likely more than she had counted on.

'What are you going to do?'

'I don't know anything right now.'

'Is there anything *I* can do?'

'Yes, you can kill her for me.'

He went to the liquor cabinet and took out a bottle of cognac and a brandy snifter. He balanced the glass in his hand and then suddenly he threw it full strength, smashing it against the living-room wall, glass splattering all over the room. He had never done anything like that before. For a second or two it felt good. But not wonderful. He swept up

the pieces before he went to bed, which gave him something
to do.

Joanna phoned him in the office the next morning and he
did not take the call. She phoned again later in the day and
he did not take the call then either. She left word for him
with the secretary: 'Tell Mr Kramer nothing has been
resolved.' Joanna had said there are courts of law and that
she had legal recourse. Ignoring her phone calls, he realized,
was not a very strong legal position.

He went to see the lawyer, John Shaunessy. The lawyer
wrote down what he considered the crucial facts, verified
some dates – how long she had been out of the house, when
she was last in New York.

'She's got a lot of lateral movement,' he said, always the
football man. Then he wanted to know exactly what Joanna
had told Ted and he jotted her remarks on his pad.

'Okay, Ted, what do you want to do?'

'What are the legal ramifications?'

'You sound like a lawyer. The law is not the issue. What
counts is what *you* want to do. Do you want to keep the
kid and live the way you've been living? Do you want to give
up the kid and change the way you've been living?'

'I hear a little judging in your voice.'

'Not at all. Ted, you win by winning. But you've got to
know if you want to be in the ball game.'

'I want my son. I don't want her to have him.'

'That's an answer.'

'She's not entitled to him.'

'Ted, that's not an answer. She's right, you know? There
are courts of law, and up to now she's been acting very
responsibly.'

'How can you say that?'

'Tactically – in her game plan. My guess is she's got somebody advising her. She hasn't made any rash moves, she hasn't
gone around you. She set herself up, established residence,
and in your home state. She said she doesn't want to shut
you out. It's all very calculated.'

'What do I do if she calls again?'

'Tell her you need a little time. She probably doesn't want to go into court unless she has to.'

'Well, I'm not giving in – '

'Ted, take the time. There's something I do which is very helpful in complex matters. I draw up the pros and cons on an issue. I actually write them out and I look at them. You should do the same.'

'I know what I want.'

'Do me a favour. Make a list of the pros and cons. And after that, if you're really sure you want to retain custody – then I'll know it's what you want, and so will you, and we'll go in there and whip their asses.'

Although he had confidence in Shaunessy, Ted wanted to be certain about him. Jim O'Connor had told Ted that he had a cousin on the bench, and Ted asked O'Connor to make inquiries and find out what he could about Shaunessy's reputation. The calls from Joanna were still unanswered. He reached her and said he needed time to weigh 'her request,' choosing his words carefully, not knowing if she were noting everything he said and taking it back to *her* lawyer. Joanna asked if she might see Billy.

'No, Joanna. It would create too many problems at this time. I don't want you to.'

'Fabulous. Am I supposed to go to court to get permission to buy my son a hot dog?'

'Listen, honeylamb, I didn't get you into this situation – you did. By the way, how come you're still using the name Kramer?'

'I just like the way it sounds. So I kept it.'

'You sure are a natural spirit.'

He hung up on this note of acrimony. So much for the reconciliation he had created unilaterally. O'Connor uncovered that of the lawyers who specialized in family law, John Shaunessy was very highly regarded. Ted set aside the question of lawyers and attempted to direct his attention to the other aspects of his life – do his job, be a father, a lover, none of which he accomplished with much effectiveness. He kept his appointment with Vivian, declining to discuss the question of Billy, although she offered to have him unburden himself. 'Not tonight,' he said. 'I've been thinking too much about it as is.' They went to the movies, a comedy, which he watched with the same mirth one might bring to an Ingmar Bergman movie. Afterwards, at her apartment he made love to her with all the passion of a wind-up toy.

The next night, at home in the middle of the night, he awakened with a start, sweating. He got up and walked into Billy's room. The boy was sleeping soundly and for the first time in Billy's life, Ted woke him from a dead sleep.

'Billy, Billy,' he said, shaking him. The child looked up with drowsy eyes. 'I love you, Billy.'

'Oh, I love you, too, Daddy. Good night.' And the boy turned and went back to a sleep he had never really left, and from which he would not remember this in the morning.

'Good night, Billy.'

Charlie had been asking Ted to meet his new 'girl-friend,' he called her. He was having a Sunday afternoon cocktail party and he wanted Ted to come. He was not really in the mood for Charlie's usual – bologna on Ritz crackers, but then he was not in the mood for much of anything. Billy had been asked to a friend's house for the afternoon and Ted could go to the party with the knowledge there would be so many of Charlie's dentist friends on the premises that he would get expert advice if he got any bologna caught between his teeth.

Charlie greeted him in his bachelor killer clothes, a leisure suit with a scarf around his neck. He walked Ted past the dentists, who were attempting to dance slow fox trots with the young women in the room, a mating ritual that seemed out of place at three in the afternoon on a Sunday in an overheated apartment. At the bar, which Charlie had set up with white wine and a new liverwurst and Ritz crackers combo, Charlie introduced him to a tall, sultry woman.

'This is my gal. Sondra Bentley – Ted Kramer.'

'Charlie has told me about you, Ted. How you're good playground chums.'

'That's us. Kings of the swings.'

He was suppressing a smile – that old Charlie managed

find such a striking woman, knowing it was patronizing him. Charlie excused himself to answer the doorbell, and if she were reading his mind, Sondra accounted for herself.

'He's not a very sophisticated guy – Charlie. But he's very sincere.'

'Yes, he is that. He's a good man.'

The women looked very young, the dentists were swarming, he did not wish to learn any more of the Sondra-Charlie relationship – that Charlie might be doing expensive dental work, free – which was his cynical suspicion. He excused himself and went into the bathroom, and lacking anything to do, he washed his face. He came out, leaned against wall watching couples dancing to 'In the Wee Small Hours of the Morning' in the middle of the day. A sexy woman in a satin blouse and dungarees, in her thirties, which made her among the oldest women in the room, stood next to Ted.

'Which side of the family are you on?' she said.

Rat-a-tat-tat. Party talk. If he came up with a good rejoinder, they were in business for the next series of one-liners.

'I'm the groom's father.' Feeble, but she laughed anyway.

'Are you a dentist, too?' she asked.

'No, I'm a patient.' And she laughed again.

Across the room, Sondra slipped her arm inside Charlie's and was whispering intimacies in his ear. Perhaps she was genuine. In any case, Charlie was free to explore the Sondras of the city, with or without free dental work, free to throw his party. Ted had never made a Sunday cocktail party, not that he would have thought it desirable, but if he ever wanted to, he would have to plan it around his son. He had about an hour to himself before he would have to call for him. Ted started working on a double depression. He was depressed about being at this party and depressed that he had to leave.

'I said, what kind of patient – was that dental or mental?'

'Dental or mental? Good. I actually sell advertising space. Look, I only have an hour. I don't think we could accomplish much in an hour.'

'What happens then? Are you a junkie? Do you have
walk your dog?'

'You're a pretty lady, but I have to go. If the way I fe
was a flood, I'd probably qualify for federal funds.'

She laughed again and he felt as if he were on a treadmi

'I got a million of 'em,' he said weakly.

He offered his goodbyes to Charlie and Sondra and we
to reclaim Billy. He did not believe he was any more ti
to his child than any other single parent, not any more
than Thelma. But more so than any man he knew, since
the divorced men he had ever met simply left the childr
to the mothers. When he took Billy home, the boy had
emotional collapse from fatigue and an oncoming col
refusing to eat anything but pound cake for dinner: 'I
good for you. It's made with eggs. I saw it on televisio
Then he started to cry because he missed a segment
Batman three days before, finally going to sleep after gaggi
on his cold medicine and spitting it all over his pyjam
unaware that on advice of counsel he might be under scrutin

Ted could not imagine resolving the question of whether
not to fight for custody of your child by drawing up a l
of pros and cons, but his lawyer seemed to believe it wou
clarify their position, so he took a pad and pen to see whe
a list could possibly lead him.

Loss of Freedom was the first reason he could think of f
not keeping Billy. Thousands of divorced men were tooti
around, the Charlies, mildly conscientious about their fe
prescribed week-end hours with the children, men who cou
go home whenever they were off duty to whatever beds th
chose to sleep in.

Sleep, a half-serious entry, was next. Without Billy
could say farewell to the twenty-four-hour day, get up
nine on a Sunday morning, possibly even nine-thirty.

Money. Undoubtedly Joanna would sue for child suppo
But she would probably be working, and he would fight h
on paying for the expense of her housekeeper. He guess
that any settlement would end up costing him less than bei
the sole bankroller of this enterprise.

Social Life. His social life had been awkward and he cou

ot, in conscience, make Billy the villain of the piece. Ted
new he was having difficulty in his relationships. It was just
o much more difficult with Billy and the constancy of his
resence.

Emotional Dependence. He and Thelma had discussed this
how parents alone with children might use the children
s an excuse not to socialize and to hold back. They decided
ome dependence was inevitable, simply from living in close
uarters with another person. But he wondered if the depen-
nce had been spilling into *Social Life*, which could not with-
and many spills.

Acceptance for Billy. He would be with his mother, as
ildren of divorced parents usually are. He would not be
rdened with explaining his parents as he grew older. He
ould be more like other children. The child needs a mother,
arriet had said, and Billy's mother was available for a phone
ll.

When he began to write down the reasons for keeping
m, the ideas did not flow as easily.

Professional Benefits, he wrote just to get started. Ted be-
ved the fact that he had to take care of Billy had made
m more responsible and more successful in his work.

He tried to think of something else and he could not. He
as blocked. He could not come up with any other reasons
r keeping Billy. No reasons. Nothing rational. Only feelings.
he hours together, the long, tiring, intimate hours of the
vo of them. How he tried to reconstruct a life for them
ter Joanna left. How they tried to come through it together.
he funny stuff. The difficult times. The injury. The pizza.
he part of his life that the boy inhabited in his own special
ay.

He *is* part of my life now. And I love him.

Ted took the list and he crumpled it up in his hand. And
en he began to cry. It had been so long since he cried, it
lt strange to him. He could barely remember what crying
as. And he could not stop.

I won't give you up . . . I won't give you up . . . I won't
ve you up . . .

CHAPTER SIXTEEN

The lawyer advised Ted to begin compiling the names of people who could vouch in a courtroom for his integrity and his fitness as a parent. He was to inform Joanna of his decision and then wait to see if she actually filed for custody. Escape was tempting. To avoid a conflict and leave her searching for them, as he and Billy went off somewhere to a simpler life, back to nature. But he had no nature to go back to, except for St James Park in the Bronx. And he was rooted in the urban condition. They could not live on berries.

He called her at the Grand Central Racquet Club.

'Joanna, can you talk?'

'Yes.'

'I've made my decision, Joanna. I have no intention now, in the future, in this life, or in any other life of letting you have Billy. There is nothing you can say or do that will convince me otherwise. I am not giving him up to you.'

'Ted –'

'We have not always spoken the same language. I hope I'm making myself clear to you.'

'Ted, I was not a bad mother. I just couldn't handle it. I know I can now.'

'And we just indulge you until you get it right? You are something. You flit in and out –'

'I'm in New York. I'm staying here.'

'Because it would look good in a custody hearing? Joanna, you want to be a mother? Go be a mother. Get married and have kids. Don't get married and have kids. Do whatever you want. Just leave me out of it. And leave my kid out of it.'

'I gave birth to him. He's my child.'

'You chose to ignore that, as I recall.'

'I even named him! Billy was *my* name for him. You wanted to name him Peter or something.'

'It was a hundred years ago.'

'You'll still see him.'

'Yes. Every night. You tell your lawyer what I said.'

'What are you leaving me to say? I'll see you in court?'

'That's up to you. I'll tell you this. If you go into court, ou will not win. I'll defeat you, Joanna.'

He hoped she would give up when she saw how resolute e was. He was bewildered once because she had gone away. low he hoped she would just go away again.

If Ted Kramer had wanted a reward for this commitment e was making to his son in the form of a dutiful, compliant hild, all he received was a 'Daddy, you stink!' in an argu- ent over bedtime. Then just as suddenly, Billy would merge from his bedroom, and not for manipulative effect, erely as a piece of unfinished business of the day, he would iss his father on the cheek, saying, 'I forgot to kiss you ood night. I mean, you kissed me, but I didn't kiss you,' nd then pad back into his room, with Ted amused, wonder- g what it could be like living through this into the teen- ge years, wanting to be there, hoping he had scared her off r that she had changed her mind, having realized how a hild could cut into her court time.

'm out of a goddamn job? Goddamn dumbbells!'

'I'm sorry, Ted,' O'Connor said. 'I'm the one who got you to this.'

People in the company had gone into huddles on why it ent wrong. Ted did not participate – he knew why. The agazine had been under-financed by company directors ithout the knowledge to see the venture through.

'I'm really thinking of retiring now, Ted. But I promise ou – I'll work on getting you a job before I think about yself.'

'Thanks, Jim. But I intend to have a job within forty- ight hours.'

'How the hell are you going to do that?'

'I don't know.'

everal vindictive employees, furious about the company's eing dissolved just before Christmas – with no bonuses and

two weeks' severance pay – stole everything they could carry
from the office: staplers, carbon papers, typewriters. Ted left
his desk exactly as it was, not even straightening his papers.
When he finished talking to O'Connor, he said goodbye to a
few people and walked right out of the office.

'Merry Christmas!' an underweight Santa Claus with a
bell and a chimney said to him outside the building.

'Humbug!' Ted replied. 'I always wanted to say that.'

The boy at the résumé service might have thought he was
deranged, this man scribbling away at a résumé on a folding-
chair next to the mimeograph machine.

'I want this in one hour!'

'Sir, it has to go to the typist and then – '

'One hour! I'll pay triple.'

While waiting for the résumés, he started phoning for
appointments at employment agencies.

'You tell him he has to see me at three today or I'll take
my business elsewhere.'

'You must be a real hot shot.'

'I am, I am.'

This was the worst time of year to be out of work –
businesses were distracted by the holidays, people were not
changing jobs. He picked up the résumés, ran from employment agency to employment agency the rest of the afternoon,
took a cab to the business office of *The New York Times* to
check all the want ads for the past week. The next morning
he was out of the house by eight-thirty, tapping his foot nervously when the subway slowed between stations, running up
the subway steps to be the first at one employment agency
so that he could be among the first at the next employment
agency. He ran, he phoned, he dropped off résumés. He
would get a job. He would get a job *fast*. He did not stop
long enough in his running to realize he was terrified.

In the first twenty-four of the forty-eight hours he had
manically prescribed for himself, he discovered the space
sales job market consisted of two jobs: *Packaging World* –
the oily publisher had never filled the job, or else he had fired
someone already – and *McCall's* magazine, where the position

had been open for two months. The job was suspect, the employment agent confided. Perhaps they were not serious about hiring. He was in a public phone booth, tapping his foot, a nervous tic he had just acquired at age forty.

'John, I haven't heard from her yet.'

'Maybe you toughed her out,' Shaunessy said.

'I guess I should mention – my situation has changed. I lost my job. The place went under.'

A long pause, too long for Ted.

'That's okay. We can handle it. If we go to a hearing, you're good for the money. I'll bet on you. And you can always pay it out, Ted.'

'Just how much can this run me?'

'It's costly, Ted. And it depends how long a hearing goes, assuming we go to a hearing. Say, in ball-park figures, five thousand.'

Joanna, will you get out of my life!

'It could cost you for her fees, too, if you were to lose, but let's not think about that.'

'Jesus, John!'

'What can I say? That's what it costs.'

'Well, what do you think about my being out of work? That can't be in my favour. Here I want to hold on to custody and I'm not even working.'

Another long pause.

'We're better off with you working. Have you got any prospects?'

'Even as we speak. Thanks, John,' as his foot tapped away.

He ran out of the phone booth towards the next employment agency and then stopped. He had been to that agency earlier. He was on the corner of Madison Avenue and 45th Street, breathing heavily, his foot tapping.

He had pushed the employment agent to set up an appointment at *McCall's* magazine for that day at 4 p.m. The advertising manager was a man in his late forties, his mind apparently on the clock and on the holidays. He looked like all he wanted to do was run through the paces on this interview. Ted sold. He sold the man on his background at the other magazines, with facts and figures on markets, demographics, print advertising compared with other media, which he remembered from a sales presentation, and then when he had succeeded in making the man a prospect, he caught him off balance by asking if there was anyone else he was required to see and could they do it right away?

'Our ad director. But he's going out of town.'

'Could you bring him in here, please? Or could we go in to see him?'

'That's a bit forward of you, Mr Kramer.'

'Well, I want this position.'

The man looked Ted over for a moment, then left the room with the résumé. Ten minutes later he returned with another man, who was in his fifties. They shook hands and the advertising director leaned back in a chair.

'So you're the go-getter?'

'Could you run through your pitch again?' the advertising manager said.

Ted went down the line with his self-sell, this time starting to close in on the sale.

'I understand you're paying twenty-five to twenty-six. That's twenty-six, I presume, for someone with my experience.'

'Twenty-five,' the advertising director said, tactically.

'Okay. Tell you what I'm gonna do, to coin a phrase. I'll take the job for twenty-four, five. That's five hundred less than you're willing to pay. Only, you have to say yes, right now. Not tomorrow or next week or after the holidays. It's worth it to me for a yes right now, and I'll take five hundred less. I plan to make it up in commissions.'

'You're a tough salesman, Mr Kramer,' the advertising director said.

'Today only. A one-time offer. Twenty-four, five.'

'Would you excuse us?' the advertising director said, and he motioned for Ted to wait outside the office.

Holy shit; I'm out of my mind. What am I trying to get away with? I must be desperate. I *am* desperate.

They asked Ted to come back in, the advertising manager took a last look at Ted's résumé.

'We'll check out a couple of your references,' he said.

'Go right ahead. Please.'

'But I'm sure they'll hold up.'

'Mr Kramer,' the advertising director said, 'Welcome at twenty-four, five.'

I pulled it off! Good God!

'Well, gentlemen, I'm very pleased to be with you.'

He rushed along the street back to the building where he *Men's Fashion* offices were located. The skinny Santa Claus was at his post, ringing a bell in front of his little chimney. Ted dropped in change, a five-dollar bill, and in excitement shook his hand so hard Santa Claus moaned.

Operations were low-keyed at *McCall's* over the holidays, and he had an easy adjustment to being in a new office. His foot had stopped tapping. He was in the flow of an established organization, and by the first working day after New Year's, he was making a full round of sales calls. He had gotten the new job so quickly the severance pay was untouched, funds earmarked for any possible custody hearing. He still had not heard from Joanna.

The phone rang one night after ten o'clock.

'Mr Kramer, this is Ron Willis. I'm a friend of Joanna's.'

'And?'

'I thought I might help in this impasse.'

'I was not aware of an impasse.'

'I thought if you and I got together, I might be able to clarify some points.'

'Are you Joanna's lawyer?'

'It happens I am an attorney. I'm not Joanna's attorney.'

'Then who are you?'

'Just a friend of hers. I think I can spare you and Joanna some discomfort if we met.'

'Somebody calls to spare me discomfort. I suppose this is the next move she's making.'

'It's not like that, believe me.'

'Why should I believe you?'

'Joanna didn't even ask me to call.'

'And she doesn't even know about this, right?'

'She does. But it was my idea.'

He was nearly as curious to meet Joanna's 'friend' as he was to learn what the other side was planning.

'All right, Mr Willis. Meet me outside Martell's, 83rd and Third, Friday at eight. We'll have a beer and we'll have a chat.'

'Very good, Mr Kramer.'

'Yes, it's all very wonderful, isn't it?'

John Shaunessy did not object to a meeting with a third party, since it could bring them information, but he cautioned against having a drink in a bar. A cup of coffee in a well-populated coffee shop would be preferable, or a pleasant little conversation in front of Ted's building. The point was not to get entrapped – into an argument, a fist-fight, a homosexual advance, and not to get arrested. He apologized for the seaminess of his outlook, but he wanted to stress that such tactics were not unknown, and that a judge might not look kindly on any of these offences.

The next morning, Ted could not believe what Billy said to him. Were children psychic? He had been careful to discuss the situation only when Billy was asleep. From nowhere, while waiting for a light to change on the way to school, he said:

'When will I see my mommy again?'

'I can't tell you that for certain.'

'I'd like to see my mommy.'

'It's hard, Billy, I realize it.'

They walked along in silence. When they reached the school, the boy looked up at his father, having just worked something out for himself.

'Mrs Willewska is sort of like a mommy. She's not really a mommy, but she's sort of like a mommy. You know what I mean?'

'Yes. You're a super kid, William Kramer.'

Presuming he had properly reassured his father, the boy went up the steps to school.

In the evening, Billy requested a story, *The Runaway Bunny*, a picture book about a little bunny who wants to un away, and his mommy bunny, against all odds, always inds him. After Joanna left, Ted discarded the book. Reading it to Billy would have been unbearable for Ted. He said hey did not have it any more and read old Babar instead. Before falling asleep Billy was talking to himself, a fantasy onversation between a mommy and a boy. Ted could no onger keep the boy, whom he loved, from seeing his mother, vhom the boy wanted to see. He called Joanna at work the ext day, a cold, brief conversation between strangers. Ted vould arrange it with the housekeeper. They set up a five 'clock dinner date for Billy with his mother on the following ight. Ted also said her friend should meet him in front of he building and not at the bar for that appointment of theirs. It wasn't my idea,' Joanna said. 'So I've been told.' And hey had nothing further to say to each other.

Ted was standing in front of the building waiting for oanna's spokesman. He arrived by taxi, a tall, blond, mus-ular young man – Ted did not think he could have been nore than thirty years old – with a tan, wearing a suit and e and carrying a light raincoat over his arm, which was ither rugged or stupid, since it was 20 wet New York egrees.

'Mr Kramer, I'm Ron Willis. Where can we talk?'

'Right here.'

'If that's how you'd like to do it. To begin with, Joanna nd I are good friends.'

'Congratulations.'

'I think I know her well. In some ways, better than you, you can accept that. I believe Joanna is a changed person ince you knew her.'

'Congratulations to her.'

Ted hated him. He hated him for his looks, his way of naintaining eye contact as though to overpower the other erson with his unsurpassed self-confidence, and he hated im for sleeping with his ex-wife.

'We got it together after she'd been through her California eriod, so to speak. She worked at Hertz, she did part-time lericals, odd jobs. She was into some self-help therapies, ome men. Nothing permanent.'

So Joanna was having trouble sustaining relationships also. Ted took some small solace from that.

'But I knew she wasn't just another California crazy. We get a lot of them.'

'I guess they come for the raisins.'

Ted was not going to make it easy. He did not consider the man his friend in any way.

Willis, who had put on his raincoat, began to shudder from the cold, and now that Ted realized Willis was not attempting to impress with his ruggedness, he considered it senseless to continue this on the sidewalk. He suggested they adjourn to a nearby coffee shop, where Willis gulped down a hot chocolate, having lost the duel of the blood.

'Can you handle bluntness, Mr Kramer?'

'Oh, please. And call me Ted, if you're being blunt.'

'I think she had a really lousy marriage with you. It got screwed up in her head, the marriage and the baby. I think Joanna over-reacted and she realizes it now. She made too big a break.'

'The lady wanted to be free. That was her decision.'

'You know, the night she first told me about the boy, she cried for three hours. It was like a dam bursting – the revelation of this child she had been hiding from me, and from herself.'

'He's difficult to hide.'

'Look, Joanna's had a chance to be on her own. And now she's discovered something. That she made a mistake. She over-reacted. Would you want to live with a mistake if it could be rectified?'

'Maybe this one can't be. Ron, you obviously don't know shit about New York weather, and maybe you don't know shit about Joanna. She's had it easy –'

'You call what she's lived through easy?'

'Listen, all she has to do is say "Sorry," and she's got somebody like you ready to back her up. Tell me, are you going to marry her?'

'What's it to you? Are you her father?'

That much was clear. He did not care for Ted either.

'We've been together for six months.'

'How sweet.' Ted felt like putting him back out on the sidewalk in his raincoat.

'I decided to come East, set up our New York office and be with Joanna to help her do this.'

'And you're supposed to talk me into it?'

'I thought I could help. It sounds like you two don't have any communication any longer. Ted, you'd have visitation rights. And consider this – Joanna would be a wonderful mother because of what she's done. She really chooses this now.'

'I'm not convinced.'

'Maybe you're uninformed. If she goes to court, you're going to lose.'

'I don't think so. My lawyer doesn't think so.'

'That's his job. You think you can go into court and prove someone who looks like Joanna is unfit?'

'Maybe I'll prove that I'm fit.'

'Ted, it's time consuming, it's expensive, it's a strain on everybody, and it's very unpleasant. I don't want Joanna to go through an experience like that if she doesn't have to. And I don't give a damn about you, but just as a human being, I don't see why you should have to go through with it either.'

'Ron, everything you say about everything may be true. But you haven't convinced me on one very important point. Why should I give up somebody I care so much about? You'd have to be his father to know what I mean. I'm his *father*. If he were my runaway bunny, I would find him.'

Joanna left a message with Ted's secretary. 'May I see Billy, Saturday at eleven, return at five?' Ted called back and left a message with her switchboard, 'Okay for eleven.' On Saturday, she buzzed and he sent Billy down. At five, she buzzed and she sent Billy up. They never met. The child passed between them.

Billy seemed happy with the day. Joanna's parents had come into town, and they went with Joanna and Billy to the zoo. Ted felt he could live with this situation, however impersonal. Billy could stay with him as he had been and

Joanna could still see her son. On Monday morning after
he left Billy at school, a man walked up to him on the street.

'Mr Kramer, I have been instructed to give you this.'

He slapped a subpoena into his hand. Joanna Kramer was
taking Ted Kramer to court to gain custody of the child.

CHAPTER SEVENTEEN

In the case of *Kramer v. Kramer*, Joanna asked the court in
her petition to overlook her original decision to leave the
child in the custody of the father. She said the decision had
been made 'under the mental anguish of an onerous marriage.'

'After making restorations to my physical and emotional
well-being,' she stated, 'accomplishing this through a change
of locale, I returned to New York City, where I now reside
and am employed. At the time that I conceded custody of my
child to the father, I was not in a stable period of my life.
I erred in conceding custody. To err is human. To be of
sound mind, of good health, of economic self-sufficiency and
for a mother to be deprived by a mistake of daily contact
with her son is inhuman. My son is only five years of age
and needs the special care, the nurturing only a mother can
provide. As the boy's natural mother, drawn back to my child
by deep and profound feelings, I ask that I be granted custody. I ask that the warmth and good spirit the child has
already shown in our recent times together continue to
flourish, with neither mother nor child deprived of the close-
ness and naturalness of their love.'

'Real direct,' Shaunessy said. 'They're going right at it—
motherhood.'

Ted Kramer spent three hours in John Shaunessy's office,
the lawyer working for his fee, taking his client through a
course in custody proceedings. The first step would be to
answer the petition and argue that custody should not be disturbed. In Shaunessy's view this was unlikely to be success-

ful, since the judge had already allowed the papers to be served. A hearing, he believed, was inevitable.

The custody hearing, as Shaunessy described it, would be similar to a trial, an adversary proceeding conducted before a judge. Each side would be permitted to call witnesses, with direct examination by counsel and cross-examination by opposing counsel. After hearing closing arguments, the judge would reserve decision, and in a few days or a few weeks, a judgment would be made as to who would be awarded the child.

As they went over details of the marriage and discussed possible witnesses, Ted lost his grasp of it. That he was actually sitting in a lawyer's office mapping strategy for keeping his son seemed monstrous. The words grew distant. He was not concentrating.

'Ted?'

'There's no way to hide, is there?' as he came back.

'Not if you want him. Some people just default.'

'No.'

'Well, you've got the ball. She's got to take it away from you.'

Shaunessy knew Joanna's lawyer, whose name was Paul Gressen. He regarded him as very able. The judge, a man named Herman B. Atkins, he considered 'A pretty humane guy.' The hearing would cost Ted $5000, win or lose – and a similar amount, perhaps, if Joanna should win and he had to pay her court costs. What was the price of a child? he wondered. Ted would find the money. He knew that. Paradoxically, the person with the price tag on his head, with his imprecise knowledge of what anything cost, would not have been able to distinguish between the cost of his new winter jacket and the cost of keeping him.

The winning or losing of William Kramer would be determined by the court under the traditional legal principle of 'the best interests of the child.' 'What we've got to do, Ted, is show that the best interests of the child is *you*.' They explored Ted's fitness as a parent, with qualities he would not have listed for himself as redeeming – that he was not an alcoholic, drug addict, homosexual or ex-convict, that he was employed, which he certainly *had* considered, and that he was not guilty of 'gross moral turpitude.'

He was not even guilty of casual sex, he realized. Vivian his most recent person, had been unavailable to him the few times he called of late. He wondered if this was because of her apprehensions over his difficulties or because of his remoteness as a result of them. But he could not stop to examine it any further, a matter which seemed so insignificant now.

From his layman's position, Ted presumed the fact that Joanna left was a compelling point against her, but Shaunessy explained *Haskins v. Haskins*, an important decision with a mother giving away custody and then wanting the child back. The judge established a precedence for awarding the child to the mother, ruling in the case that 'Motherhood is not so easily abdicated.'

Shaunessy's sense was that Joanna might be vulnerable on the issue of her history, that her comings and goings might hold some weight emotionally, but the main argument as he saw it was to be Ted Kramer. Ted was a responsible, dedicated, loving father, and the best interests of the child would not be served by having him taken from his father's care.

'Plus I think we take a run at her mental stability. Did she ever talk to the walls?'

'Joanna?'

'Ted, this is a dirty game we're in. They'll use anything they can against you. So think dirty. Good for us if we can show she was a little off her keester for running out, even if she wasn't certifiable.'

'She never talked to the walls, John.'

'That's too bad.'

In thinking of people who might stand up for him, he wondered if his housekeeper could be a witness. She knew Billy better than anyone and had observed father and son at home, but he hesitated in asking her. The woman was so unsophisticated, putting her on the stand seemed to be exploiting her, as he suggested to Shaunessy.

'Come on, Ted. Get into the game. You put your pet para

keet up there if he can say something on your behalf.'

'She's just a very innocent lady.'

'Sign her up. We'll coach her.'

But Etta Willewska was confused by the nature of the proceedings.

'Mrs Kramer wants to take Billy away?'

'Well, she has the right to try.'

'He loves you so much.'

Come on, Ted, get yourself into the game.

'Mrs Willewska, would you be willing to say that in court?'

'To speak in front of people?'

'Yes. To tell them how we live here.'

He asked the lawyer about Billy. Does *he* go into court? Is he a witness? For which side?

'No, Ted. The judge might want to talk to him in chambers, but I doubt it. The boy is *non sui juris*. Too young to testify. He's incompetent.'

'Just so he doesn't know it,' he said, relieved.

Ted had chosen not to inform Billy that his parents were about to go into court to fight over him. And he said nothing at work. He was caught in a cycle on his job – if he became too preoccupied with the hearing, he could risk losing his job, and if he lost his job, he could risk losing the hearing.

On the return date of the petition, he went down to the courthouse, finding the time between sales calls. Shaunessy told Ted his appearance was unnecessary, that normally the lawyers argue these motions without their clients present, but Ted did not want any of this to happen without his knowledge, and he met his lawyer outside a room in the matrimonial part of the courthouse. Joanna was absent from the proceedings, leavng her lawyer to attempt a quick manoeuvre before the judge. The lawyer moved that Joanna's petition be complied with on the force of her statement, that custody be given to her with no hearing required. The judge, a small, bald man in his sixties, swatted it away with the same ease that he dismissed Shaunessy's plea that no hearing be required, and that custody should not be disturbed.

Paul Gressen was a suave man in his late forties, wearing a smartly shaped suit with a matching silk handkerchief and

tie. He had a soft voice and an ironic smile, which he used
tactically. John Shaunessy was not to be outlawyered in pose
or tailoring. He was a tall, imposing figure with his grey hair
and his own courtroom uniform, a three-piece blue suit with
a white carnation in his lapel. But in the end, the lawyers'
poses and their legal manoeuvring did not alter what Shaunessy had predicted earlier would be the result – a hearing. The
judge expressed his interest in expediting the matter, due to
'the young age of the child.' He then set a date for the hearing
to be held in three weeks.

Shaunessy stepped out into the corridor with Ted and apologized for not leaving with him, but he had other clients'
business to conduct here. They would talk in the morning.
Ted, alone, headed for the lobby and walked down the steps
of the courthouse, to be hereafter considered by the court
as 'the respondent' in the action brought by 'the petitioner.'

The judge appointed a psychologist to investigate the respective homes and personalities of the parties in the dispute.
The psychologist came to Ted's apartment on a week-day
night, a chubby lady in her forties who never smiled. Dr
Alvarez walked through the house, opened cupboards, the
refrigerator, bedroom closets, the bathroom medicine chest.
She asked if Billy could play in his room for a few minutes,
and she took out a clipboard and pen to interview Ted. She
wanted to know how he spent his day, how his time with Billy
was distributed, what activities they shared together, what
he did when he was alone, did anyone else stay in the house
with him. He mentioned Etta, but the intent of the question
was purely sexual, which he learned when she followed up by
asking directly:

'Mr Kramer, do you have sex here with anyone?'

When I can, lady. Did you have anything in mind?

'Doctor, I attempt to conduct my social life discreetly.
At the moment, I am not seeing anyone in particular.'

'Does that distress you?'

'Not unduly.'

'What does?'

'Distress me?'

Your being here, this hearing, Joanna, her lawyer, the judge, being judged on the most fundamental part of what I am.

'I don't know how to answer that. The normal things that distress people. The cost of living, my child being ill . . .'

'Very well. I'd like to talk to the child, if I may. Privately.'

In the doorway of Billy's room, he had a metropolis in progress, toy cars being driven by superheroes, his leather belt as a highway, blocks stacked into buildings, all of which prevented the door from being closed. Ted was able to listen from the living-room.

'What do you have here, Billy?' she asked.

'Detroit.'

'Have you ever been to Detroit?'

'No, but I've been to Brooklyn.'

Ted was curious if she was writing all this down.

She asked him what his favourite games, activities, people were. For people he mentioned Kim, Thelma, Mrs Willewska, Daddy, and Batman.

'What about your mommy?'

'Oh, sure. My mommy.'

'Do you like to be with your mommy?'

Ted began to get uncomfortable. He wanted to break in and tell her she was leading the witness.

'Oh, sure.'

'What do you like best about her?'

'Lunch in a restaurant.'

'And what do you like best about your daddy?'

'Playing.'

'Tell me, does your daddy ever hit you?'

'Lots of times.'

This brought Ted right outside the door.

'When does he hit you?'

'When I'm bad.'

Billy, what are you doing?

'He hits me on the Planet Kritanium when I steal the buried treasure from the famous peanut butter factory.'

'In real life when does he hit you?'

'My daddy doesn't hit me, silly. Why would my daddy hit me?'

The interview ended right there. Dr Alvarez said good-bye, took a last look at the environment, and the night concluded for Ted and William Kramer with the flying of Fred Flintstone in Batman's plane into Detroit.

On a Monday, the day before the hearing, Ted went in to see the advertising manager at work and said he needed a few days off, they could take it from his vacation time, but his ex-wife was contesting the custody of his child. He had held off telling anyone in the office in order to eliminate gossip or doubts about him, and now he would have his job through the hearing. He went through his work day, making sales rounds, diffidently now, his ability to be attentive breaking down by the hour. At 5 p.m., he went home to his son, who still did not have any sense that the following morning at nine-thirty, *Kramer v. Kramer* was on the court calendar.

On the façade of the courthouse it said, 'The True Administration of Justice is the Firmest Pillar of Good Government.' Good government? All I want is my boy.

Ted Kramer entered the courtroom for the hearing. When he looked around, he was very moved, seeing the people there, his people who had come to help. Thelma, Charlie – God, Charlie, what is it costing you to be here? – Thelma and Charlie sitting next to each other, joined for this moment by Ted's need, Etta, wearing an Easter bonnet of a kind, Larry's wife, Ellen, who thought that because she was a teacher her presence might be useful, Sandy, his sister-in-law, who had flown in from Chicago, and Jim O'Connor with a haircut and a new shirt and tie, all here out of love to help him keep his son.

Joanna entered, looking beautiful in a wool knit dress, accompanied by Ron Willis and her lawyer. She and the lawyer took places at the table facing the judge's chair. Ted began to move forward to join his attorney at their table when the door opened and in came Joanna's parents. They

looked away from him in what appeared to be deep embarrassment. His former in-laws were here apparently to testify
against him. They took seats to the back, on the other side of
the family.

The room was stately, a high ceiling, oak benches and
mahogany furniture in good condition, 'In God We Trust'
on the wall facing the courtroom, an American flag to the
side. The judge arrived in his robes, the guard announced,
'All rise!' the stenographer took his place in front near
the witness chair and they were ready to begin. Ted took a
long, probing breath, searching for air.

Joanna as the petitioner had the right to the first round, and
her lawyer placed her on the stand immediately as a witness
in her own behalf. They would not be bothered building a
case with secondary characters. Motherhood, the mother, was
their main argument, and her persona was placed in evidence.

Joanna's testimony began slowly, her lawyer carefully
established dates, an outline of the years with Ted, and then
with Billy, up to the present. Ted found himself remember-
ing – wild stray thoughts, the first time he and Joanna made
love, this beautiful woman whom he no longer knew, wrapped
her legs around him. The first time he held Billy, how tiny
the boy seemed. The first time he watched Joanna breast-
feeding the baby. She did breast-feed him. That would not be
in the testimony. He had forgotten that.

Gressen then began to ask Joanna about her job and her
responsibilities at work. He linked this to an earlier time.

'Mrs Kramer, did you ever work in a job while you were
married to your ex-husband?'

'No, I did not.'

'Did you wish to?'

'Yes.'

'Did you ever discuss with your ex-husband your desire to
work?'

'I did. He said no. He strongly objected to my working.'

They began to focus on Ted, a man who resisted his
wife's personal growth. They were seeking to justify Joanna's
leaving. Ted *had* said no to her working. It did not seem

possible to him that he could have been so narrow. He could hardly recognize himself from the testimony. Yet he knew he had been that person they were describing, even though since then he had changed. The judge called a lunch recess, and Ted watched Joanna conferring with her lawyer. He wondered if she, too, had changed, if there were two different people in this room than had been in that marriage, and what if they were attracted to each other, what if they met now, as the people they were now – would they end up in this room?

Shaunessy began to gather together paper that was on the table in front of them – copies of the petition, the psychologist's report, paper all around, the stenographer's record spilling out of his machine like a long tongue, note paper, legal documents.

Joanna was the first to leave the courtroom with her lawyer. After a diplomatic delay so they would not be in the same elevator, Ted left the room with his lawyer – the petitioner separated from the respondent by people, by paper, by legal jargon, by time, as they took a recess from this stately courtroom, this marital graveyard.

CHAPTER EIGHTEEN

Joanna's lawyer continued to work on the apparent soft spot in her case, the fact of her leaving. He was attemping to convert it into a strength – that her decision was evidence of the depth of her frustration, caused by the respondent, who had left her no choice.

'Would you tell the court, did you enjoy playing tennis?'

'Yes.'

'And your ex-husband, how did he respond to your enjoyment of tennis?'

'He resented it. He called himself a tennis widower in front of people.'

Emotionally confined, she found herself with the additional

burden of a small child.

'Did you love the child?'

'Very much.'

'When he was an infant, how did you feed him?'

'I breast-fed him. So I could be closer to him as a mother.'

This was not a circumstance where one side overlooked any possible advantage.

'And yet you chose to leave your child?'

'My predicament was overwhelming. If my husband had been open to my having my own interests, I would not have been in such despair.'

'That's only true in part,' Ted whispered to his lawyer. 'She didn't *have to* leave.' Shaunessy nodded. He had been here before. 'I even asked that we seek help.' 'Shhh,' the lawyer said and placed his hand on his client's arm to reassure him.

'Everything became one – the marriage, my husband, the pressure, the child. It was all one to me because it was one. My husband had cut off my options.'

'And what did you do next?'

'I took the only action I could see for myself under the circumstances. Since everything was one to me, I couldn't pick the parts out of the whole that needed to be fixed. I had to free myself of the whole, of all of it. And I left to make a better life for myself.'

'So you gave up your child?'

'No, not my child per se – my marriage, my husband, my frustration, and my child. I was leaving this entire package my husband had tied up so tightly.'

'Mrs Kramer, why have you set up residence here in New York?'

'Because the child is here. And his father is here. As a mother, I don't want my child to be separated from his father.'

'Goody two-shoes,' Shaunessy muttered to his client.

Gressen queried her as to the time when she first began experiencing a sense of loss regarding the child. She fixed this at the morning after her leaving.

'What did you do about this sense of loss?'

'Nothing then. I hadn't purged myself yet of my frustrating marriage experience.'

'Objection. The witness is giving an opinion.'

'Sustained.'

'Did you ever call your husband to express your feelings about the child?'

'Yes, I did. Christmas, a year ago.'

Gressen introduced into the record Joanna's telephone bill, which listed phone calls made to Ted from California, and Joanna stated that the purpose of the calls was to arrange a meeting with the child.

'What did your ex-husband say about this meeting?'

'He was hostile to it. At first, he said he would have to let me know. Then when he consented, he asked me if I intended to kidnap the boy.'

'Did you kidnap the boy?'

'No. I bought him a toy he wanted.'

The psychologist's report was placed in evidence. Dr Alvarez had not drawn any negative conclusions on either side. Joanna was characterized as 'self-assured' and the environment she planned for the child was 'suitable for the child's needs,' which the lawyer used as testimony to Joanna's fitness. Then the circumstances of her last meeting with Billy were recounted, Joanna telling how pleased the boy was to be with her.

'Did the child say that in so many words?' Gressen asked.

'Yes. He said, "What a really good time this is, Mommy." '

Billy's enthusiasm had been introduced as evidence.

Finally, Gressen asked her, 'Can you tell the court why you are asking for custody?'

'Because I'm the child's mother. You said to me, Mr Gressen, when we first met, that there were instances when mothers were granted custody of their children even when they had signed away custody. I don't know the legal wisdom of that. I'm not a lawyer, I'm a mother. I know the emotional wisdom. I love my child. I want to be with him as much as I can. He's only five. He needs me with him. I don't say he doesn't need his father. He needs me *more*. I'm his mother.'

Gressen had worked his client and the clock. Joanna's

testimony had run to four-thirty in the afternoon. Judge Atkins called a recess for the following day, leaving the case on behalf of motherhood, delivered by a poised attractive mother, to stand unchallenged overnight.

'Don't worry, Ted,' Shaunessy said. 'Our case is still you. But we'll try to move her some tomorrow.'

Direct examination by the petitioner's lawyer was essentially a series of prearranged questions to arrive at a conclusion agreed upon by lawyer and client. Joanna was less poised under cross-examination. Where Gressen's style was sly, Shaunessy worked from the position of the gruff, older wise man. He cut into Joanna's testimony, made her account for the blocks of time that had passed after she first left to the Christmas phone calls, from the Christmas meeting to her most recent return.

'When you originally left, and you had this sense of loss you referred to, did you send the child letters, gifts?'

'No, I –'

'Did you send anything?'

'I was still living through my experience with my husband.'

'You sent the child nothing at all to express your love?'

'I sent them in my heart.'

'In your heart. Did this small child grasp the symbolism?'

'Objection. Counsel is attempting to intimidate the witness.'

'Can we hear the question again?' the judge said to the stenographer, and Ted leaned forward in his chair. Was the judge not listening? Was he sitting up there, his mind drifting while this important issue was being decided? Or did he want to make certain of his ruling? He was the judge, though. He could do anything he wanted in his courtroom. The stenographer read back the question.

'Over-ruled. The witness can answer.'

'All I know is that Billy has always been happy to see me.'

'How long do you plan to live in New York, Mrs Kramer?'

'Permanently.'

Shaunessy picked up on the word permanently, using it as a weapon.

'How many boy-friends have you had – permanently?'

'I don't recall.'

'How many lovers – permanently?'

'I don't recall.'

'More than three, less than thirty-three – permanently?'

'Objection.'

'Over-ruled. The witness will answer, please.'

'Somewhere in between . . .'

Shaunessy had told Ted, there was little to be gained from making an issue of a mother's promiscuity, unless it was extreme, which they would have difficulty proving. He obviously had other intentions here.

'Do you have a lover now?'

'I have a friend.'

'Is he a lover? Do we need a definition of terms, or are you the Virgin Mary?'

'Objection!'

'Sustained. Mr Shaunessy, do you really expect an answer to a question of that nature?'

'I would request a direct answer to the direct question, Does she at present have a lover?'

'I'll allow that. The witness will answer, please.'

'Yes.'

'Is that permanently?'

'I . . . don't know.'

He pressed on. How many jobs had she held permanently, what had she done permanently, when she went to California was that permanently, when she came to New York to see the child was that permanently, when she went back out to California was that permanently, when she came back to New York was that permanently? He was taking a run at her stability and Joanna was faltering, she began to stammer, she became vague, 'I didn't . . . know at the time . . .' She lowered her voice so that the judge had to ask her to speak up.

'We don't really know, then, do we, when you say permanently, if you're really planning to remain in New York or even keep the child, for that matter, since you've never really done anything in your life that was continuing, stable, that could be regarded as "permanently"?'

'Objection! I must ask that Counsel be prevented from harassing the witness!'

'Well, there is an admissible question in there,' the judge said. 'Do you intend to remain in New York permanently, Mrs Kramer?'

'Yes,' she said quietly.

'I have no further questions at this time.'

Gressen was entitled to a re-direct examination of the witness, and he carefully reconstructed their motherhood position – 'mother' their key word; 'As a mother, I felt . . .' 'Being a mother, I could tell . . .' used through by witness and lawyer as if to trigger an automatic response in the judge. They went over the steps Joanna had taken to gain custody of the child, her return to New York, her search for a job, her finding an apartment where 'As a mother . . .' she knew Billy would be comfortable, the legal procedures she undertook – hiring the lawyer, filing the petition, down to appearing in court on this day – all because of her longings as a mother, details presented to prove the deep commitment to a young child by a stable, responsible mother.

Shaunessy had a last re-cross-examination.

'Mrs Kramer, how can you consider yourself a fit parent when you have been a failure in virtually everything you have ever undertaken as an adult?'

'Objection!'

'Sustained.'

'I'll ask it another way. What is the longest personal relationship you have ever had in your life other than parents and girl-friends?'

'I'd have to say – with my child.'

'Whom you've seen twice in a year? Mrs Kramer, your ex-husband – wasn't he the longest personal relationship in your life?'

'Yes.'

'How long was that?'

'We were married two years before the baby. And then four very difficult years.'

'So you were a failure at the longest, most important relationship of your life?'

'Objection.'

'Over-ruled.'

'I was not a failure.'

'What else do you call it? A success? The marriage ended in a divorce!'

'I consider it less my failure than his.'

'Congratulations, Mrs Kramer. You have re-written matrimonial law. You were *both* divorced, Mrs Kramer!'

'Counsellor, do you have a question of the witness?' the judge asked.

'I'd like to ask what this model of stability and responsibility has ever succeeded at. Mrs Kramer, were you a failure at the longest, most important personal relationship of your life?'

She sat silently.

'Please answer the question, Mrs Kramer,' the judge said.

'It did not succeed.'

'Not it – *you*. Were *you* a failure at the most important personal relationship of your life?'

'Yes,' she said barely audibly.

'I have no further questions.'

Joanna left the witness stand, looking exhausted.

'Motherhood is tough to score against,' Shaunessy said to his client. 'But we drew blood.'

After a lunch recess, the hearing continued with Joanna's father, Sam Stern, taking the stand for the petitioner. His function for Joanna was to serve as an eyewitness to the mother-son relationship. Gressen restricted his line of questioning to this one area, with an even narrower emphasis on the recent Saturday when Joanna took Billy for the day, and Sam and Harriet joined them. As he heard Sam describe the pleasant afternoon and the ease with which Joanna dealt with her child, Ted realized he had been had. That day was an ambush. The grandparents had been there for the specific purpose of providing this particular testimony. Shaunessy attempted to cross-examine, but he could not make inroads on the limited testimony. This is what the man saw with his own eyes – mother and son got along very well.

As he came off the witness stand, Sam tried to slip past Ted at the table without looking at him. Ted reached out for Sam's arm.

'Sam?'

Sam Stern's head was down. Without ever looking up, he said, 'Ted, you would do the same for your child, wouldn't you?' and he moved on quickly.

Gressen did not call any other witnesses. He had assembled a highly compact case. Motherhood was the main issue. The mother was the main evidence.

The arguments for the respondent began. Charlie was the first witness, Shaunessy referring to him constantly as 'Doctor' to give more weight to the testimony. The doctor vouched for Ted's character and for his excellence as a parent.

'Would you trust your child in his care?'

'I already have. Many times.'

He described outings in the city with the children, his first-hand observations of the boy's affection for his father, and the father's for the boy. With emotion in his voice, he said, 'I don't think I could have been as good a father in these circumstances.'

Gressen declined to cross-examine. With a smile, he virtually dismissed the testimony as inconsequential. He adopted the same tactic after the testimony of the next witness, Ted's sister-in-law, Sandy, who described Ted's concern for Billy's welfare, which she had observed, and said, 'The boy adores him.' Thelma took the stand next and was overwrought. When Shaunessy asked her:

'What have you been witness to that would attest to Mr Kramer's competence as a father?'

'Their relationship,' she said and she nearly cried.

'Objection, Your Honour. The answer is, to be generous, rather vague.'

'Sustained.'

'Can you recall any particular incident that relates to Mr Kramer's care of his child?'

'He reads to Billy, he bathes him, he plays with him, he loves him, he's a very kind man . . . and if you ever saw them together . . . there wouldn't be a trial at all . . .' and she started to weep.

Shaunessy said he had no further questions. Gressen looked for a second as though he might like to move in on her, but a man who was building a case on motherhood must have thought better than to confront a mother's tears and he declined to cross-examine.

Jim O'Connor said Ted Kramer was 'highly regarded in his field' and 'a man I deeply respect.' When he had completed his support of Ted as a competent, respected professional, Gressen decided to not let this witness pass.

'Mr O'Connor, this person you say was so excellent in his work and such an outstanding professional, didn't you fire him – twice?'

Ted spun around to look at Shaunessy. Where did they get that information?

'Not exactly,' O'Connor said.

'What exactly?'

'The companies failed. We were all terminated.'

'Even our miracle worker here?'

'Objection!'

'Sustained.'

'I have no further questions.'

Ellen took the stand, and speaking as an elementary school teacher testified that Billy's brightness and spirit, which she had been witness to, came as a result of Ted's excellence as a parent. Gressen let her pass. Shaunessy then placed in evidence the psychologist's report, which held a positive view of the respondent, as well – the apartment was 'comfortable for the child,' and Ted was deemed 'a competent parent.'

Etta Willewska was called. Shaunessy asked a series of questions about her observations of the household. Nervous, uncertain of language, she spoke in simple terms of the atmosphere in the house. 'He is a very sweet boy.' 'You should see how he loves his daddy.' 'I could take him to school, but they like to be together.'

Gressen, concerned about this testimony, decided to cross-examine.

'Mrs Willewska, you are in Mr Kramer's employ, are you not?'

'Excuse?'

'He pays you, doesn't he?'

The sarcasm that he was developing, that she had been bought for her remarks, escaped her entirely.

'Yes, but my sister takes care of Billy today while I am here.'

'This man gives you money, doesn't he?'

'Yes, but I don't know about today,' she said, confused. 'Maybe he should pay my sister.'

When the lawyer noticed both the judge and the court stenographer smiling at the unassailable naïveté, Gressen withdrew, rather than engender more sympathy for the witness.

'No further questions,' and he mustered a slight smile of his own in Shaunessy's direction, professional respect – You got me on that one, John.

Ted Kramer was to be next, the final witness in the hearing. They would begin in the morning.

At nine-thirty, the testimony began. It ran for the length of that day and through half of the next. What passed in the courtroom was a description of nothing less than a man's life. They went back to the time of Joanna's departure, to the decisions he made to keep the boy, to find a housekeeper, to keep the household stable, on through the day-to-day concerns of being with the child, winter viruses and a small boy's social life, rainy Saturdays and 4 a.m. monsters. Shaunessy's questions were delivered with feeling and compassion, as though a career of handling the niggling arguments of people in hate had suddenly been elevated by this one client who had become his cause. Give the man his kid, he seemed to be urging the judge. Look at what he's done. They covered the long week-ends, the clothes bought, the books read, the games played, the constant commitment, the depth of his caring, and somewhere in the closing hours of the testimony a change took place in the courtroom. Joanna Kramer, who had sat without expression throughout, modelling her indifference after her lawyer's, began to listen, drawn into the testimony, the accumulation of detail, unable to take her eyes off the witness. Ted Kramer answered the last question – as to why he wanted custody, and he said, 'I have no illusions about it, or that my boy will be grateful. I only want to be there, as I have been, because I love him.' A recess was called prior to cross-examination, the judge withdrew to his chambers, and Ted Kramer came off the stand, embraced by his lawyer and his people.

In cross-examination, Joanna's lawyer began to fire questions at Ted about hours, days, nights spent away from Billy, how often did Ted hire baby-sitters, leave the child to sleep with women, the lawyer attempting to impugn the witness on both his morals and his commitment to the child.

'I don't think, and do you agree, that we should add in as child care the time when you're home and the child is asleep?'

'You're on duty then, too.'

'Unless you have a woman in your bed then, too.'

'Objection!'

'Sustained.'

'Mr Kramer, have you ever had a woman in your bed while your child is in the next room asleep?'

'I suppose.'

'So do I.'

Ted thought it was crude, an attack of innuendo and half-truth, but his lawyer had taken a low road with Joanna also, and it was as Shaunessy had said, a dirty game. Gressen now attacked Ted's employment record with dates and places. Ted realized now that they had hired a private detective to find information to use against him. 'How many months was that, Mr Kramer?' 'How many jobs does that make in the last two years?' What Ted had believed was an achievement, finding work, the lawyer was trying to turn into a character defect by stressing that Ted had been out of work in the first place.

'I'm at *McCall's* now. I don't believe they are going out
business.'

'How long have you been there?'

'Two months.'

'We'll give you time.'

'Objection, Your Honour!'

'I'm only examining the man's employment record, Your
onour. He pretends to fitness when he cannot hold a job.
the witness wishes to challenge these dates –'

'Are they accurate, Mr Kramer?'

'Yes, but that's not the whole –'

'I have no further questions.'

In his re-direct examination, Shaunessy sought to reinforce
s client's position, wasn't job turnover endemic to the field,
dn't he improved his professional status over the years,
asn't an adult social life and the hiring of baby-sitters
mmon practice, and wouldn't he go home that night after
e hearing and administer to his child's needs as he had been
ing all along since his ex-wife's abandonment?

The petitioner's lawyer had the opportunity for one final
-cross-examination.

'Mr Kramer, did your child nearly lose an eye when he
as in your care?'

For a moment, Ted could not absorb the question. They
ere bringing up the accident.

'I say, Mr Kramer, did the child injure himself while he
as in your care and is he now permanently disfigured?'

Ted Kramer suddenly felt physically ill on the stand. He
oked over at Joanna. She was holding her face, her hands
overing her eyes.

'Objection, Your Honour. Counsel is raising a question
at is not germane to these proceedings.'

'While the child was in the care of the witness, he cut
s face badly and is now scarred.'

'Are you introducing the question of negligence here,
ounsellor?'

'Yes, Your Honour.'

'I see. Well, you'll have to do better than that. Do you
ave any affidavits to support negligence?'

'I do not, Your Honour, however –'

'This is an isolated incident, Counsellor, unless you c̱
prove otherwise.'

'Does the witness deny the injury took place?'

'No, Counsellor, I'm going to overrule you on this line
questioning.'

'Then I have concluded my questions.'

Ted stepped off the stand, still feeling ill. He walk
slowly towards Joanna and stood in front of her.

'The lowest, Joanna. The lowest –'

'I'm sorry,' she said. 'I just mentioned it in passing.
never thought he'd use it.'

'Really, now?'

'Believe me, Ted. I never would have brought it up. Neve

But the events simply had gotten beyond her. Both sid
had their lawyers, the lawyers had their tactics, the lawye
and the tactics had a life of their own. And now both sid
had hurt and had been hurt.

The custody hearing ended with the closing arguments ł
the lawyers, a summation of all the key points in their clien
positions. The petitioner and the respondent would not spe
again in this courtroom, not to the judge nor to each oth
Counsel for the petitioner argued for motherhood, 'th
unique, life-giving force,' he said, 'compared to which nothi
on earth is more basic.' As part of his argument he said
was 'unnatural to separate a child so young from its moth
unnatural for the child to be with his father when the moth
is so obviously fit, ready and able to give a mother's spec
love and caring.' Counsel for the respondent argued f
fatherhood. 'Father love is a powerful emotion,' he said.
can run as deep as a mother's love, as we have seen in t
testimony in this courtroom.' And he argued for, specifica₥
the fatherhood of Ted Kramer. 'It would be cruel and unju
to overturn custody in this case,' he said at the end of ł
argument. 'Custody should remain in the warm home of
loving father, a man whose fitness for custody has be
proven by the very conduct of his life.'

And it was over. The judge would decide. He wou

analyse the testimony, be guided by the facts and the law, and make his decision. There would be no dramatic climax to the proceedings. People of furrowed brow would not wait to hear the decision, gripping the sides of tables, as in court-room movies. The decision would not be given in the court-room. It would be published routinely in a law news paper, the newspaper would be delivered to the lawyers, the lawyers would telephone their clients. The announcement of which parent could keep the child would be cold, anticlimactic in style – but it would be binding.

CHAPTER NINETEEN

He did not permit himself to ever be more than fifteen minutes out of reach by phone. He was also running a switch-board for other people's anxiety. Among the callers, his mother was phoning daily from Florida.

'Did you hear yet?'

'I'll let you know.'

'You let me know.'

'Mother, you're not reducing the tension. Maybe you should call her.'

'Her? I wouldn't call her. I'll call you.'

He relived the custody hearing, second-guessed his law-yer's strategy, critiqued his responses on the witness stand, and in the end, he was satisfied with the presentation of his case.

During these days following the hearing, he performed in the manner that had been described in the courtroom, which was the normal conduct of his life. He spent his days at work and his evenings at home with his son. But the hours passed more slowly than any time he had ever known, more slowly than any time of his being unemployed, even more slowly than his first three weeks at Fort Dix when his orders had been misplaced and he remained in the reception centre, officially in the Army, but not – time that did not count towards basic training. This was similar, worse – time that did not count towards anything but getting to the judge's decision.

A three-day week-end was approaching for Washington's Birthday, and Larry and Ellen offered to open the house on Fire Island. Since there was no water or heat, they would camp out in the house and use sleeping bags. Billy called it 'a big adventure,' and for Ted it would be a chance to pass a long week-end and get to the next business day, when he would begin to wait again for the lawyer to call.

As the time for the trip grew near he was becoming less enthusiastic about spending his nights in an unheated summer cottage by the ocean in the winter, but Billy was very excited, making certain he had fresh batteries for his flashlight so he could see skunks and raccoons outside the house at night, sharpening his plastic scout knife to do battle with wild bears. Ted amused himself with the possibility of a retrial on the basis of new evidence, freezing one's ass off for one's child.

On Friday, the day before the week-end, his lawyer called.
'Ted, it's John.'
'Yes?'
'The decision is in, Ted.'
'Yes?'
'We lost.'
'Oh, Jesus –'
'I can't tell you how sorry I am.'
'Oh, no.'
'The judge went for a motherhood ruling straight down the line.'
'Oh, no. I think my heart is going to break.'
'I'm upset, too. I'm very sorry, Ted.'
'How could she win? How?'
'She's the mother. Ninety per cent of the time, they give it to the mother. It's even higher with little children. I figured this one time, just this time, we could sneak in there.'
'No!'
'It's terrible.'

'I lost him? I lost him?'

'We tried, Ted.'

'It isn't fair.'

'I know.'

'It isn't fair, John!'

'Here. Let me read you the decision. It's a very traditional ruling, I'm sorry to say.'

' "In the matter of *Kramer v. Kramer*, the petitioner is the natural mother of the child, William, five and a half years of age. The mother in this proceeding seeks custody of the child from the father, in whose custody the child had been placed one year and a half ago in a prior divorce action. The court is guided by the best interests of the child and rules the best interests of this child, who is of tender age, will be served by his return to the mother.

' "The petitioner now resides in Manhattan and has taken steps to create a suitable home for the child. Prior determination of custody is not considered by the court to be conclusive, *Haskins v. Haskins*. The mother, having experienced stress at the time of the marriage, now shows every sign of being a competent, responsible parent. The father is also deemed a competent, responsible party. As between fit and proper parents, the court must make the best available choice, *Burney v. Burney*. The court rules the best interests of a child this young, *Rolebine v. Rolebine*, dictates a finding for the petitioner.

' "Ordered, adjudged and decreed that the petitioner be awarded care and custody of the minor child, effective Monday the 16th of February. That the respondent pay for the maintenance and support of said child, four hundred dollars each month. That the father shall have the following rights of visitation: Sundays from eleven a.m. to five p.m.; and two weeks during either July or August. No costs." And that's it, Ted.'

'That's it? What do I get, Sunday from eleven to five? That's what I get with my boy?'

'At least you don't have to pay her court costs.'

'What's the difference? I lost him. I lost him.'

'Ted, you'll still be in his life if you want to be. Sometimes the parents fight like hell for custody, and the one who loses doesn't keep up, and never sees the kid that much.'

'Either way, we become strangers.'

'Not necessarily.'

'Monday – it starts Monday. That's right away.'

'It's not exactly permanent. If conditions should change, you could always bring a petition against her.'

'Sure.'

'We can also appeal. But you still have to comply. And they usually sustain.'

'So I just turn him over, right? I just turn him over?'

'Ted, I'm so sorry. I honestly believe we gave it our best shot.'

'My Billy. My little Billy. Oh, Jesus –'

'I don't know what else we could have done –'

'Terrific. And now the one who's supposed to be unfit to keep him – *I'm* the one who's in charge of telling him. Oh, Jesus –'

Ted Kramer left the office for the day, too sick in spirit to work. He went home and rummaged through Billy's room, trying to determine how you managed it. Did you pack up his entire life in boxes? Did you leave pieces behind for when he might come to visit? He tried to plan what he could say to him, how you explained.

Ron Willis, serving as an intermediary for Joanna, called after trying to reach Ted in the office. He was courteous on the phone, the party assuming power being gracious to the losing side. He wanted to know if Monday morning at ten would be convenient and if Ted could put together a suitcase or two of Billy's key possessions. They could arrange for any other toys or books later on.

Etta returned from food shopping and Ted informed her that Joanna had been awarded custody of the boy. The time she had spent with Billy had been invaluable, he said, and Billy would always have a good foundation from the love she had given him. He had decided to make a request of Joanna that she retain Etta as a housekeeper, and Etta said of course she would be willing to take care of Billy. Then she got busy in the house, putting away food. A little while later he heard her. She was in the bathroom, crying.

Billy was to be finished with his school day shortly, and Ted asked Etta to take him to the park for a while. He had unfinished business and he could not bear to see him just now. He began making phone calls to tell people, hoping to reach secretaries, third parties, answering machines, preferring to just leave messages and not have to get into conversations. He thought it would be best to leave the city for the weekend as planned, for Saturday and Sunday anyway. Ted could get away from the phone, and Billy would be deeply disappointed if the adventure were cancelled. After he left his messages, spoke to friends, shared their regrets, he called his mother. Dora Kramer did not now as he expected she might. 'Joanna won custody,' he told her, and she said quietly, 'I was afraid of that.'

'Will I never see him again?' she asked, and Ted was not clear for the moment how visitation rights worked for grandparents.

'I promise you, Mother, you'll see him. If nothing else, on my time.'

'My poor baby,' she said. He was about to answer her with some invented reassurance about Billy, when she said, What will you do?' and he realized his mother was referring to him.

The question of Etta was an immediate concern to Ted. He wanted to get to Joanna before she made plans. If he mailed a special-delivery letter immediately, Joanna would have it in the morning. He did not care to speak to her. There were other things to be communicated about Billy, as well. He could not pin a note to his jacket as though the child were a refugee. He wrote:

Joanna – This is by way of introducing William Kramer. He is a sweet child, as you will see. He is allergic to grape juice, but will more than make up for the loss in apple juice. He is not, however, allergic to grapes. Don't ask me why. He seems to also be allergic to peanut butter from the health food store, fresh ground, but not the stuff they sell in the supermarket – and don't ask me why. At times, in the night he will be visited by monsters, or one particular monster. It is called The Face. The Face, as best I can determine, looks like a circus clown without a body, and from what the pediatrician says, and what I have read, may be a sexual fear of losing his penis, or a fear of his own anger, or just a circus clown he saw once. His doctor, by the way, is Feinman. His best medicine for colds is Sudafed. His best stories have been Babar and Winnie the Pooh up to now, with Batman moving up. His housekeeper has been Etta Willewska and is a main reason for this note. She is a loving woman, conscientious, very concerned about Billy, experienced, anything you'd want in a housekeeper. Most important, Billy cares for her and is used to her. I hope you don't feel the need to make such a clean slate that you won't consider her. I urge you to retain her. Her number is 555-7306, and I think she will take the job if offered. I'm sure other things will come up. Ask me what you need to and I guess eventually we'll talk. That's all I can think of right now. Try to speak well of me in his presence, and I will try, against my feelings, to do the same for you, since it would be 'in the best interests of the child,' as they say. Ted.

He mailed it special delivery from the post office and then went home to wait for Billy. The boy came into the house, his face rosy from the outdoors. He rushed to Ted – 'Daddy, you're home so early,' hugging his father around his waist. He could not tell the boy then that he no longer lived there, nor could he tell him at dinner, a last Burger King, or at bedtime, with Billy turning out all the lights to test his 'super-powered raccoon-spotting flashlight.' Ted delayed through breakfast the next day, and finally, unable to put it off any longer, while waiting for Larry and Ellen to call for them, he made the speech.

'Billy, you know your mommy now lives in New York City?'

'I know.'

'Well, sometimes when a mother and a father are divorced, there is a discussion about who the child should live with,

e mother or the father. Now, there is a man who is very
se. He's called a judge. And the judge has a lot of experi-
ce with divorces and mothers and fathers and children. He
cides who it would be best for a child to live with.'

'Why does he decide?'

'Well, that's what he does. He's a very powerful man.'

'Like a principal?'

'Bigger than a principal. The judge sits in robes in a big
air. This judge has thought a lot about us, about you and
 and Mommy, and he has decided that it would be best
 you if you live with Mommy in her apartment. And I'm
y lucky. Because even though you live with Mommy, I'll
 to see you every Sunday.'

And I will, Billy, I promise you. I won't be one of those
ple Shaunessy talked about.

'I don't understand, Daddy.'

Neither do I.

'What part of it don't you understand, honey?'

'Where will my bed be, where will I sleep?'

'At Mommy's. She'll have a bed for you in your own room.'

'Where will my toys be?'

'We'll send your toys there, and I'm sure you'll get some
v ones.'

'Who will read me my stories?'

'Mommy.'

'Will Mrs Willewska be there, too?'

'Now, that I don't know about. That's still being discussed.'

'Will you come and say good night to me every night?'

'No, Billy, I'll still live here. I'll see you on Sundays.'

'I'll live in Mommy's house?'

'And it will all start this Monday. Your mommy will come
 you in the morning and pick you up here.'

'But we were supposed to go for the week-end! You
mised!'

'We'll still go. We'll come home a day earlier, that's all.'

'Oh, that's good.'

'Yes, that's good.'

The child took a few moments to evaluate the information,
n he said:

'Daddy, does this mean we'll never play monkeys again?'

Oh, Jesus, I don't think I can get through this.

'Yes, my honey, we'll play monkeys again. We'll just b
Sunday monkeys.'

On the car ride to Long Island, the grown-ups worked desper
ately for a jolly beginning to the week-end, singing 'I'v
Been Working on the Railroad' and other favourites. In th
interludes between the forced merriment, Ellen would glanc
back at Ted and Billy and then turn away, unable to look
Given the slightest break from the songs, everyone above th
age of five and a half was solemn. Billy was talking away
fascinated by the off-season life on the island: 'Where d
the birds go?' 'Do children live there?' 'Does the ferry crasl
into the ice like an icebreaker boat?' and then he, too, woul
fall silent, thinking.

'Daddy, I have a secret.' And he whispered so the other
would not hear. 'What if The Face comes when I live a
Mommy's?'

'Mommy knows about The Face. You and Mommy wil
tell The Face to beat it.'

On the ferry ride across, Billy looked out the window
not wanting to miss even a wave in his adventure, and the
his interest would drop, apprehensions would take him ove
again.

'Does Mommy know I can't drink grape juice?'

'Yes, she knows. She won't give you anything that's n
good for you.'

When they reached the island, Billy converted the empt
summer houses into 'Ghostland,' creating a game which l
and Ted played through the morning, searching for ghost
climbing on and off decks of houses, scaring each othe
laughing. Don't make this too wonderful, Ted was thinkin
Maybe it's better if we go out on a shitty time.

The child's enthusiasm was infectious. After lunch, Lar
and Ellen, lightened by the rum the adults had been drinkir
on this cloudy, cold day, played Ghostland also. Then th
all jogged along the beach. After dinner, Billy took his flas

;ht out to look for small animals, but Ghostland was sud-
nly legitimate. He lasted outside in the dark for only ten
inutes, driven indoors by shadows and night sounds.

'Did you see any deer?' Larry asked. 'There are deer on
e island, you know.'

'Not in Ocean Bay Park,' Ted said. 'They won't rent to
em.'

They began to laugh, Billy also, who thought it was very
nny.

'Can you imagine if the deer shopped in the grocery?'
lly said, a joke by a five-year-old, and on laughter and
m and the long day outside, they all fell asleep in their
eping-bags, chuckling to the end.

Sunday, the last day, Ted and Billy bundled up and went
wn to the beach to build a sandcastle. The beach was
apty. They were on an island of their own this one last time.
ey tossed a ball on the beach, took a walk to the bay and
t on the dock, finally going inside to get away from the
w weather. Ted and Billy played pick-up sticks, the boy
tent on the game, and then as before, his mind began to
ift again. He suddenly turned and looked at his father
th lost eyes. Ted Kramer knew that he had to be the
ddy now, no matter how deep his own pain, he had to help
e boy get through this.

'You're going to be fine, Billy. Mommy loves you. And I
ve you. And you can tell anybody just what it is you want,
natever it is.'

'Sure, Dad.'

'You'll be just fine. You're surrounded by people who love
u.'

On the ferry back, no one was laughing any more. For
d, the pain of their separation was so intense he could
rdly breathe.

In the city, Larry and Ellen dropped them off at the house.
ang in, buddy,' Larry said to Ted. Then Ellen kissed Billy
d told him, 'You're welcome to visit us on the island
y time. You remember that. We'll look for deer in the
cery.'

'It will have to be on a Sunday,' the boy said, graspin the reality completely.

Ted saw that Billy brushed his teeth, got into his pyjama then he read him a story. He said good night, keeping cheery. 'See you in the morning, Billy.' He tried to watch movie on television, but he was, thankfully, exhausted. An then he took one final look at the boy sleeping. Had he i vested too much in the child? he wondered. Perhaps som what, he thought. But as he had come to believe, a certai amount of this was inevitable when you were alone with child. Joanna would find it the same. He decided it was just it should have been during these many months. He wa grateful for this time. It had existed. No one could ever tak it away. And he felt he was not the same for it. He believe he had grown because of the child. He had become mor loving because of the child, more open because of the chil stronger because of the child, kinder because of the child, ar had experienced more of what life had to offer – because the child. He leaned over and kissed him in his sleep and sai 'Goodbye, little boy. Thank you.'

CHAPTER TWENTY

They had several hours before Joanna would arrive.

'What do you say we go out for breakfast this mornin kiddo?'

'Do I get a doughnut?'

'After.' Ted Kramer had picked up all the parental shor hand.

They went to a neighbourhood luncheonette and sat in booth – breakfast out. Soon he would be like the other Sunda fathers, looking for things to do – out. They returned to th apartment and packed Billy's important belongings into tw suitcases. There was nothing to do now but wait for Joann Ted allowed Billy to watch morning television in Ted's be om, while he read the newspaper in the living-room.

Joanna was late. It was ten-fifteen. The least she could have
one this one day was make it as painless as possible, he
ought. By ten-thirty, he was pacing. A really shitty thing to
o, Joanna! By eleven, he realized he did not even have her
hone number. The number was unlisted. He tried to locate
on Willis and could not. At eleven-twenty, the phone finally
ng.

'Ted?'

'Goddamn it, Joanna!'

'I'm sorry.'

'Where the hell are you?'

'Home.'

'For Christ's sake!'

'Ted, I'm not coming.'

'You're –'

'I can't make it.'

'What is this, Joanna?'

'I – can't – get it together.'

'You can't get it together?'

'I can't.'

'You mean this morning, today? What the hell are you
ying, goddammit?'

'I can't . . . I just can't.' And she started to cry.

'What can't you?'

'I mean . . . sitting in the courtroom . . . hearing what
ou've done . . . what's involved . . .' He could barely make
ut her words. 'The responsibilities . . .'

'What about it? Joanna, what about it?'

'My head just isn't there.'

'Joanna, I have a boy here with his bags packed!'

'He's a lovely boy –'

'Yes, he is.'

'A lovely boy.'

'Joanna –'

'I thought it could be different. But when it comes down
o it . . . I mean, faced with actually doing it –'

'What? *What*, goddammit?'

'I guess I'm not a very together person. I guess . . . the

things that made me leave are . . . still a part of me. I don
have very good feelings about myself just now.'

'Joanna, what are you saying? Where *are* we for Christ
sake?'

'I can't make it, Ted. I can't commit to –'

'Joanna!'

'He's . . . yours, Ted.'

'He's mine?'

'I did want him. I really did –'

'Do you mean this?'

'I'm not coming, Ted. I'm not showing up.'

'Is this for true?'

'I won't fight you for him any more.'

'I can have Billy?'

'I don't think any judge would object now . . .' And sh
trailed off into deep sobbing.

'Oh, Ted . . . Ted . . . Ted . . . Ted . . .'

'Easy, Joanna –'

'You know, I guess I am a failure. I'm a failure, just lik
your lawyer said.'

'Jesus – the things we've done to each other.'

'You can have him, Ted. He's yours.'

'He's really mine?'

'Yes, Ted.'

'Oh, my –'

'Only . . . could I ask you something?'

'What, Joanna?'

'Could I see him sometimes?'

She was so vulnerable at this moment, he felt he coul
anihilate her with a word. By his just saying no, she woul
go away. But it was not in him to do so, nor did he feel h
had the right.

'We'll work something out.'

'Thank you, Ted. I . . . just can't talk any more.' An
she hung up.

He leaned back against the wall, so overcome that his leg
could not even support his weight. He sat down at the dinin
room table, numb, shaking his head, trying to believe
Billy was his. After all this, he was his. He sat there, tea

streaming down his face.

Once Etta had told him he was a very lucky man. He was feeling this now, joy and thankfulness and that he was truly a very lucky man. He got up and walked over to the packed suitcases which were standing in the foyer, and still crying, he carried them back into the boy's room.

Billy was watching television. He needed to be told. Ted tried to compose himself, then he went inside, turned the television set off and kneeled in front of the boy.

'Billy, Mommy just called. And . . . well, Billy . . . you're going to live here with me, after all.'

'Mommy's not coming?'

'Not today. She loves you. She loves you a lot. But it's going to be the way it's been.'

'It is?'

'Because I love you, too, Billy.' His eyes filled with tears again. 'And . . . I would have been . . . very lonely without you.'

'You mean I'll still sleep in my bed?'

'Yes. In your room.'

'And all my toys will stay?'

'Yes.'

'And my Batman?'

'Yes.'

'And my books?'

'Everything.'

The child tried to register it.

'So I'm not going there today?'

'That's right, Billy.'

'Are you working today?'

'No.'

'Then can we go to the playground, Daddy?'

'Yes, Billy. We can go to the playground.'

They did ordinary things that day, went to the playground, brought back a pizza, watching *The Muppets*, Billy went to bed, and Ted Kramer got to keep his son.

Fontana Paperbacks

Fontana is a leading paperback publisher of fiction and non-fiction, with authors ranging from Alistair MacLean, Agatha Christie and Desmond Bagley to Solzhenitsyn and Pasternak, from Gerald Durrell and Joy Adamson to the famous Modern Masters series.

In addition to a wide-ranging collection of internationally popular writers of fiction, Fontana also has an outstanding reputation for history, natural history, military history, psychology, psychiatry, politics, economics, religion and the social sciences.

All Fontana books are available at your bookshop or newsagent; or can be ordered direct. Just fill in the form and list the titles you want.

FONTANA BOOKS, Cash Sales Department, G.P.O. Box 29, Douglas, Isle of Man, British Isles. Please send purchase price, plus 8p per book. Customers outside the U.K. send purchase price, plus 10p per book. Cheque, postal or money order. No currency.

NAME (Block letters)

ADDRESS
